THE HAUNTING OF
Swain's Fancy

THE HAUNTING OF
Swain's Fancy

BRENDA
SEABROOKE

Dutton Children's Books

NEW YORK

Library of Congress Cataloging-in-Publication Data

Seabrooke, Brenda.
The haunting of Swain's Fancy / by Brenda Seabrooke.—1st ed.
p. cm.
Summary: Eleven-year-old Taylor spends the summer with her father and
his new family in a historic house in West Virginia and, while contending with
hostility from her stepsister Nicole, attempts to solve the mystery of ghosts
who haunt the site.
ISBN 0-525-46938-9
[1. Ghosts—Fiction. 2. Stepfamilies—Fiction. 3. West Virginia—Fiction.] I. Title.
PZ7.S4376 Haw 2003
[Fic]—dc21   2002031540

Published in the United States 2003 by Dutton Children's Books,
a division of Penguin Putnam Books for Young Readers
345 Hudson Street, New York, New York 10014
www.penguinputnam.com

Printed in USA • Designed by Tim Hall
First Edition
1 3 5 7 9 10 8 6 4 2

This one is for Ian James

THE HAUNTING OF
Swain's Fancy

CHAPTER

1

"WHAT A SPOOKY OLD HOUSE," MRS. CALLAHAN SAID. "I'D
sure hate to live in it. Gives me the shivers." She gave a fake
shiver that rattled her plastic bangles.

Taylor stared down the long driveway at the stone house
that loomed behind a pair of huge oak trees. It was two
stories tall plus an attic. The dormer windows looked like
a pair of stern, forbidding eyes staring out. Dad hadn't said
much about the house except that it was old and needed
some fixing up, and they'd been working on it since January.
Taylor hadn't expected anything this big or this old. When
the car stopped, she unloaded her suitcase and other bags
from the trunk while Mrs. Callahan made more disapprov-
ing remarks. "I bet it's murder to heat that place. I'd hate to
have their utility bills. They ought to turn it into a museum
and move to a nice modern house."

Taylor tried to think of a polite way to reply, gave up, and
carried her suitcase to the front steps. She let the heavy brass

knocker fall on the front door with a loud thump. Mrs. Callahan worked in the office next to Mom's. Mom had said they were lucky Taylor could ride with her on such short notice and that Burneytown, West Virginia, was on the way to her sister Bertha's, where she was going for the weekend.

"They don't seem to be home," Mrs. Callahan said.

"I'm sure somebody's here," Taylor said. "They're expecting me. I'll check around back."

The wing on the left side of the house had its own door. Taylor knocked, but no one answered it either. A screened porch ran the width of the back of the house. Its door was latched, and no cars were parked in the open barn beyond. Taylor didn't know what to do. She went back and stood in the shade of a tree beside the car.

Mrs. Callahan looked at her watch. "I'm going to be late for the shower." The bangles rattled on her other arm.

"I'm sure Dad or Sylvia will be back any minute," Taylor said, feeling anxious that no one was home and that she was holding Mrs. Callahan up. "There's no sense in your waiting. Why don't you go on."

Mrs. Callahan looked doubtful. She checked her watch again. "Well, I don't know. . . ."

Taylor had heard more than she ever wanted to about the baby shower during the two-hour trip from Washington, D.C. She wished Mrs. Callahan would leave. "You don't want to miss the shower. If Dad and Sylvia aren't back soon, I'll go over to the neighbor's. The . . . um . . . Adamses. They're always home."

"Why didn't you say so?" Mrs. Callahan wasted no time getting in her car. Taylor gave her a reassuring smile, the kind her mother always whipped out when Taylor wasn't sure about things, and waved until Mrs. Callahan had zipped down the driveway and turned out of sight on the county road.

Taylor was happy to be alone but annoyed at the same time. Dad knew she was coming this afternoon. So did Sylvia. Why weren't they here? Where were Nicole and Peter? What would she do if they didn't come back soon? There weren't any neighbors named Adams. She had made that up with the first name she could think of. There weren't any neighbors at all that she knew about. Taylor hadn't noticed any nearby houses along the way. If nobody came by four, she would walk to town and call her mother's cell-phone number, and they would figure out what to do. Mom could always work things out. That was her job—public relations—solving problems for a new senator from New Mexico. She'd had to leave today to solve one for him in Santa Fe, and Taylor had to come to her dad's a week early, right after school was out. That was OK with her, but why wasn't anybody here?

She tried the doorknob again. Still locked. She stepped back and looked at the heavy wooden door. Cut into the stone lintel over it were the words SWAIN'S FANCY 1754. What did that mean?

At least it was cool. Giant trees shaded the house from the hot June sun. A lawn sloped away on each side, bounded by a boxwood hedge, flower beds, and trees.

The house faced south. On one side, beyond a group of fat Christmas trees, Taylor discovered a small pond with a bridge to a tiny island, just big enough for the white-painted wooden summerhouse with its bell-shaped roof. She walked across the bridge. Minnows basking in its shade darted away, shimmering the still water. She sat on the encircling bench inside the summerhouse. The big stone house seemed to peer over the trees, watching her. Its windows were divided into a lot of little panes. Taylor counted twelve panes in the dormer windows, fifteen in each of the larger ones on the two lower floors. She could walk around and count all the windows and figure out how many windowpanes were in the whole house. It would be something to do. Or she could stay here on the little island.

A cloud of gnats found her. Taylor fanned them away and moved to the other side of the summerhouse. As she sat down, she saw something move in the upstairs attic window. A face. She bet it was Nicole. It would be just like her to hide up there and keep Taylor locked out. Nicole would think that was funny. Taylor waved but nobody waved back, and the face disappeared.

How had they come home without her seeing them? They

knew she was here. Her things were at the front door. Why didn't they look for her? Why were they watching her from the attic? Suddenly Taylor was furious. Sylvia should have let her know they were home. Or Nicole or Peter.

She ran across the bridge to the front of the house. No one was there. No car stood in the driveway. Had they slipped in while she was walking down to the pond? She banged the door knocker and yelled. No one answered. The house seemed to be waiting for something.

Or someone.

CHAPTER
2

Don't think like that, Taylor told herself. It's just a house. An old house where lots of people have lived.

And died.

Taylor backed off the porch and checked the attic windows again. Blank. The outer windows were the same. She sat on the front steps and rummaged in her bag for food, but all she found was a flattened M&M's package on the bottom. She shook it out and was rewarded with a yellow one. She let it dissolve on her tongue. Lunch. Mrs. Callahan had been in a hurry. "You can eat at your dad's," she'd said when she picked Taylor up at the apartment this morning.

Taylor wished Dad and Sylvia hadn't moved up here. Dad had lived in a town house in D.C. until their wedding a year ago. Sylvia had lived in one, too, with her kids, Nicole and Peter. They wanted to get out into the country, he said. So they bought this old house in Burneytown, West Virginia. Dad had moved up here after Christmas to work on the house. Taylor had hardly seen him since then, just brief visits in March and April, neither lasting more than two hours. Four hours with her dad since Christmas. She hadn't spent a single night with him since he had sold his town house. The others had all moved up here permanently when school let out last week. Before that, they came up on weekends to help get the house ready. Nicole and Peter got to spend every night with him. It wasn't fair. He was her dad, not theirs. Dad had apologized and said he would make it up to her in the summer.

Now it was summer. She was here and he wasn't. Taylor stretched her legs in front of her. Where was all that peace and quiet Dad had said they wanted so much they had to move to the country? The silence here was the noisiest Taylor had ever heard. Things buzzed and hummed and clacked all around her. She was used to city sounds. Cars, taxis, buses, Metro. Country quiet wasn't really quiet. It was eerie.

Maybe something had happened. Maybe she should break a window to get in. She jumped up as a car turned into the driveway and ran to the parking area to meet it. Doors opened on the small cream-colored station wagon. Sylvia stepped out, cool in a long slim green dress, her blond hair tied back with a green scarf. She smiled when she saw Taylor. Nicole got out on the front passenger side, a smaller version of Sylvia with a wider mouth that wasn't welcoming her with a smile. She wore a floaty old dress, Sylvia's probably, and had a circle of flowers around her head. Taylor felt her own dark hair, damp and droopy with sweat, hanging like wet strings.

Peter jumped out of the back of the car, his arm in a sling. He grinned proudly and held up the cast. "Look, Taylor, I broke my arm."

"Taylor, you're here already." Sylvia gave her a cheek kiss. "I'd hoped we would get back first. Peter tried to fly out of a tree."

"Mom, I did not." Peter was emphatic. "I fell out."

Sylvia threw up her hands. "I don't know what you were doing up there."

He mumbled something.

"I am the Queen of the Fairies, and he was one of my servant fairies," Nicole said, ignoring Taylor.

"I was not," Peter said. "I was Tarzan."

"Whatever," Sylvia said. "Here's Taylor to spend the summer with us."

"Hey, Taylor," Peter said. "You want to be the first to sign my cast?"

"Sure. Hi, Nicky."

"Don't call me that," Nicole said, barely moving her lips.

It was obvious that Nicole didn't want her here. Well, Taylor had news for Nicole. She didn't like Nicole any better than Nicole liked her, but they had to try to get along for the next six weeks.

"Your dad went to Winchester, Taylor. He had expected to be back before now but the water pump on the car broke and he had to get it repaired. He should be back soon. Nicole, help Taylor with her things." Sylvia went in the house.

Nicole glanced at Taylor's bags, waited until Sylvia was out of sight, then without a word brushed past Taylor and went into the house, leaving Peter to help with the bags. He carried one while Taylor struggled with the rest.

The house was cool inside and felt like a lot of people had lived here. Taylor couldn't explain it, she could only feel it. It was as if people were doing things in the rooms, people who were no longer here: cooking in the kitchen, waiting in the hall, mending in the parlor—doing all the things they did a long time ago. If she looked quickly, she might catch a glimpse of them.

The central hall was as wide as a room and had furniture in it, chairs and cupboards. The hands on the tall clock showed 1:15. "Um, where should I put my stuff?" Taylor asked.

"Put it anywhere. Put it on the ceiling, put it on the floor, put it in your pocket, put it out the door," Nicole chanted as she drifted up the stairs.

Peter giggled. Taylor didn't think it was so funny. How would Nicole feel if Taylor had treated her that way at her house?

"Sylvia, where should I put my stuff?"

"Upstairs, Taylor," Sylvia called from another room. "You're sharing Nicole's room for now. Until we can get a room ready for you. It will be fun for you and Nicole to be together. I shared with my sister when I was growing up and we've always been close, I think, because of that."

Nicole wasn't her sister. She was Taylor's stepsister, one she hardly knew. But Taylor didn't remind Sylvia. Peter was her stepbrother, and she liked him. Peter wasn't anything like his sister.

Taylor climbed the stairs, Peter behind her. He was almost as tall as she was and had brown eyes and sandy hair. More important, he liked her. Unlike his stuck-up sister.

Upstairs the hall was not quite as wide but had furniture in it, too, an uncomfortable-looking sofa, a table, and some spindly chairs. Nicole's room was at the front of the house and overlooked the pond on the side. Her furniture was all antique-looking: a double bed with tall posts, a marble-topped dresser.

"You can hang stuff in here," Nicole said, opening a door to a tall cabinet she called an armoire.

Taylor pushed the door open and saw a three-inch space. "Thanks."

Nicole stared at her. "What for?"

"For being so generous." Taylor couldn't stop her sarcasm. She didn't have much to hang anyway. She had only brought one dress. This wasn't supposed to be a dress-up summer.

"All that wonderful fresh air will be so good for you," Mom had said. "And now you'll really get to know your new stepsiblings."

Taylor already knew all she wanted to know about Nicole, a year older at twelve, unfriendly, and greedy, always taking the best of everything for herself—the best piece of chicken, the best chair, the biggest piece of cake.

Peter was a year younger. His room was across the hall. A smaller bedroom behind Nicole's had been turned into a bath and next to Peter's was the door to a spare room. Another door led to the attic. Sylvia and Dad's room was in the wing that had been added later to the house and could only be reached by its stairway from the kitchen–family room. The spare bedroom was only for show, Nicole said. "The furniture is really old. Mom got it at auctions. That's why you can't stay in it. That's why I have to share my room with you."

Taylor got the message. She was as welcome as Lyme disease. "What about the attic room?"

"What attic room?" Nicole pulled a green book from a bookcase.

"Isn't somebody staying up there?"

"No. Steve's going to turn it into rooms later on."

"But I saw somebody up there before you came."

"Nobody was here," Nicole said. "Unless you saw a ghost." She giggled and ran downstairs with the book.

"Taylor, come sign my cast," Peter said from the doorway to his room. Taylor stashed her bag. She would finish unpacking later. At least she was welcome somewhere.

Peter's room was already messy, with spaceships hanging

from a ceiling decorated with stick-on stars and constellations, maps pinned to the wall, birds' nests, rocks, movie posters, plastic things. No antiques here. He spread a fan of colored markers for Taylor to choose from.

"What's your favorite color?"

"Red," he said.

She picked different shades of red, purple, and hot pink and wrote Taylor in tall block letters up the length of his cast. She wasn't leaving much space for anybody else. That was OK. She didn't have much room in this house, but she could take all the room she wanted on Peter's cast.

"Hey, that's cool," he said as her name took shape.

Taylor colored in the letters with the hot vibrant shades, starting with red for the *T*. This was one name that would be noticed.

"I don't understand why can't I stay in the other room," Taylor said, shading the *A* with magenta.

"It's only for showing to the public during July Daze."

"What's that?" Taylor colored a cerise *Y*.

"It's a festival. People pay to see old houses on a tour. Mom has been working to get our house ready this year. She writes about it in her column 'Yesteryear Today,'" Peter explained.

"What's it about?" Taylor worked on a dark purple *L*.

"Fixing up an old house. Cleaning up old pieces of furniture. Finding out the history of old houses. Going to yard sales and flea markets. That kind of stuff."

Dad could have made a place for her in the attic, a place

of her own so she wouldn't have to bunk with a snobby step-sister who didn't like her. Taylor colored the *O* orange and finished with a red *R*.

"Cool," Peter said again, admiring it.

"Thanks. Um, Peter, do you think I could get something to eat? Mrs. Callahan didn't want to stop for lunch."

"Sure. I'm almost always ready to eat."

The kitchen, located under Dad and Sylvia's bedroom, was in the wing of the house with its own outside door. Taylor glanced at the living room as they went through the hall. It looked like a museum. So did the dining room. But the kitchen–family room was more modern, with comfortable chairs and sofa, a round wooden table, dark wooden cabinets. Baskets and old cooking utensils hung from the walls and ceiling, and potted plants grew in sunny spots. Antiquey things like copper kettles and pots and old bottles, dried flowers, wooden bowls of wooden fruit mixed with real, candlesticks, and wooden roosters were tucked around and into bookcases and gave the room a cluttery warmth. The stairway in the corner led up to the master bedroom. Another one led to the cellar below. A door connected the kitchen area to the dining room.

They made peanut butter and banana sandwiches and took them out to the island summerhouse with a pitcher of lemonade and glasses. They pretended they were marooned on an island in the South Seas. Peter was fun but when they finished eating, they were back in West Virginia with the rest of the summer waiting for them. "Let's watch TV or some-thing," she suggested.

"Can't." Peter shook his head. "No TV."

"You mean you don't have one here?"

"Yes, we have one. But we don't have cable, and we only get two and a half stations," he said morosely.

"How can you get half of a station?"

"You can see it, but there's so much snow and static that you don't want to. Mom won't have a satellite dish around the house. She says it's too far out of period, whatever that means. Steve said we might get a mini-satellite later on if he can figure out a way to rig it up without ruining the period look of the house. Anyway, Mom says TV stunts our brains."

"Got any new computer games?"

Peter gave her a look of pure misery. "No. Just my old ones. Mom says the budget is tight right now with all the work on the house."

"But this is child abuse!"

"I know. That's what Nicole told them. But they just laughed. We're supposed to play the old ones or read and explore and make up our own games. Or play board games like Monopoly or chess. With real boards and funny little things for markers and real cards. If Mom could, she would have us living in the eighteenth and nineteenth centuries. Wanna play one of the games?"

Taylor shrugged. "OK."

Peter got the Monopoly game, and they played the rest of

the afternoon on the screened porch, sitting in comfortable twig chairs with fat cushions. It wasn't much fun with just the two of them, and it took Peter forever to count out money one-handed to pay off her hotels when he landed on Park Place.

Dad came home at four, bear-hugging Taylor and apologizing profusely for not being here to meet her. "It was the water pump. I had to have the car towed. I told the mechanics I needed a rush job because my daughter was coming. They did the best they could. But now you're here for the summer, and we're all going to have a great time," he said, beaming.

Maybe summer wouldn't be too bad. At least Dad was here now, and Peter was friendly. Sylvia, too. Nicole was the only sour note. That and the two and a half TV channels. Taylor was glad they were allowed to use electricity for reading. She had been worried that Sylvia would make them use candles or oil lamps!

CHAPTER

3

NICOLE REAPPEARED AT SUPPERTIME. SHE WOULDN'T SAY where she had been. She tossed her head when Peter asked her and acted like she hadn't heard him. Taylor folded napkins carefully at each place. She wouldn't let Nicole think she was in the least bit interested in anything Nicole did.

"She has all these secret places I'm not supposed to know about," Peter whispered to Taylor when Nicole went to wash her hands. "She was probably in one of those. Maybe with Cody Jackson."

"Who's that?"

"He lives over the hill through the woods. He's in your grade, but he hangs out with Nicole all the time, never with me except when she gets mad at him. He's mostly cool."

They ate supper at the big round table—hamburgers, applesauce, and beans. Nicole hardly said a word. Dad was extra jolly as he talked about their plans for the house. "We want to use the attic for bedrooms for the family and eventually have all three bedrooms on the second floor furnished in period style."

"You can help me choose fabrics for the curtains and wallpaper for the new rooms in the attic," Sylvia said to the two girls as if that would be the most fun in the world. Nicole rolled her eyes, but not so that her mother could see her. Taylor thought it might be fun. She liked to look at wallpaper sample books.

After supper Dad played a game of Scrabble with Taylor and then she played Yahtzee with Peter. Sylvia watched the news on a TV set hidden in a cupboard. Nicole had disappeared again. Maybe to her secret place. As Peter threw the dice, Taylor noticed that the *T* she had written on Peter's cast had been turned into a fat black *C*. Nicole had written her name around the wrist part of the cast like a bracelet in chunky black letters. Now only AYLOR was left of her name.

Taylor's mother called at eight. She took the phone out on the porch to talk in private. She'd planned to tell her mother how awful everything was.

"I hope you're having fun," Mom said. "I just got here. It's only six—we're on Mountain Daylight Time—and I have about ten minutes to change for a dinner meeting."

"Yeah, I'm having fun," Taylor said. Mom was too rushed to hear the real meaning behind those words. Taylor didn't say anything more. There was nothing Mom could do about it now. She clicked off after telling her mom she loved her and went back to the game.

At nine-thirty Dad shooed them to bed. "You can read awhile upstairs," he said.

Taylor unpacked while Peter and Nicole took turns in the shower. Then it was her turn. The bathroom was decorated with more antique things: candle-lamp sconces on each side of an antique mirror, quilt-patterned wallpaper, baskets filled with soap, bottles of gel, fancy towels. Taylor was glad they didn't have to use an outhouse.

Nicole was already in bed reading. She looked up with her cat's eyes as Taylor came in wearing her blue nightshirt with the sailboat on the front. "Oh, you sleep in a T-shirt." It didn't sound like a compliment.

Taylor pressed her lips together to stop herself from saying, "And what's wrong with that?" Dad had bought her the shirt on a trip to the Eastern Shore of Maryland last summer. They had made a mistake in the size, and the shirt was enormous. "Yes," she said. "And you sleep in a long white crepe gown with lace around the neck."

"What do you mean by that?"

Taylor didn't mean anything by it. Two could play that game, saying nothing and making it sound like something. She ignored Nicole and pulled a book out of her bag. She started to get into the double bed.

Nicole sat up, glaring. "What do you think you're doing?"

Taylor froze, half in, half out of bed. "Going to bed."

"Not in my bed. You sleep over there." She pointed to a foldaway bed set up by the front windows. It was made up with flowered sheets, a pair of fluffy pillows, and a white cotton blanket, but they couldn't disguise the fact that it was a foldaway. Taylor was outraged. Why did Nicole get a bed and she had to sleep on a cot?

"I don't want to sleep with you anyway," Taylor said as she got into the cot. It creaked as she shifted on the mattress. She opened her book and looked around for a lamp. She didn't have a bedside table or a lamp. The only light came from the one by Nicole's bed. She had to hold her book at an awkward angle to read.

After about ten minutes, Nicole turned the light off without saying a word. Taylor dropped her book with a loud thump, not even marking the place. She was sleepy anyway. Outside the open windows, crickets and other insects screamed their heads off. Somewhere a bunch of frogs competed in a yelling contest and something clicked like castanets.

Taylor stared at the black rectangle of the window. She had never slept where she couldn't see a single light outside. It was scary, all that dark, even with fireflies blinking their lights on and off. The moon was rising. Or was it falling?

A circle of light seemed to descend into the darkness beyond the window. Wasn't the moon supposed to rise? Taylor sat up to get a better look over the sill beside her cot. The circle seemed to be coming closer, closer, a round shape with bluish craters in it. It must be the moon. But wasn't the moon supposed to get smaller, not bigger? It came closer.

Now Taylor could see it clearly. It wasn't the moon at all. It was a face. A white ghostly face with black eyeholes floating against the sea of dark trees beyond.

Taylor let out a scream.

The face disappeared.

Footsteps sounded on the stairs. The door to their room opened. Dad's anxious face appeared, followed by Sylvia's and Peter's. "What's going on here?"

Nicole turned on the light. "Yeah, what's the matter, Taylor?" She emphasized "Taylor."

"A face! I saw a face!" Taylor babbled.

"Where?" Dad's eyes quickly swept the room.

"There, in the window."

"This window?" Dad pointed toward the front of the house where the driveway ran to the county road.

"Yes, that one."

"Stay here." He and Sylvia went downstairs. Peter and Taylor watched from the window as Dad turned on the outside lights and walked around with a flashlight. He came back upstairs.

"Taylor, there's nothing out there."

"I saw it!"

"What did it look like?"

"It was white and ghostly and had craters for eyes."

"Maybe you had a bad dream. That's understandable in a strange place," he said soothingly.

"No, Dad, it wasn't a dream. I wasn't asleep."

"Maybe it was car lights reflecting off something. Nature causes some strange ocular projections, mirages, things like that."

"Well, maybe." Taylor wasn't convinced.

"Nicole, did you see anything?" Dad asked.

"No, I was almost asleep." Her eyes didn't look sleepy. She looked like she was enjoying the show.

"OK, everybody. Go to sleep," Dad said. He sent Peter to bed, turned off the light, and went out. Nicole snickered. Taylor turned her face to the wall, unconvinced. It wasn't funny. She HAD seen something.

But what?

CHAPTER

4

SOMETHING WAS ON HER BED. SOMETHING ALIVE. TAYLOR opened her eyes. The room was dark. She couldn't see anything. She lay still, afraid to move a muscle. Maybe the face had found its body and climbed in the window. When nothing happened, she began to move. Inch by inch she turned her head until she faced the window, but there was only blackness in the rectangle, punctuated by three late-blooming fireflies.

The thing on her bed moved. Slowly. Stealthily. It crept from the area around her feet to her knees. Could it be a rat? A giant rat that sneaked in from the barn? A giant rat with long yellow teeth and blazing red eyes? A rabid bat? A raccoon? A snake? Something worse? What could be worse than a snake?

It stopped next to her knees, then moved up by her stomach. She hoped it wouldn't bite her. Or touch her. Taylor felt pins and needles all over. If she lay still, maybe it would go away like all nightmare things do.

It didn't.

The thing crawled closer and closer. It wasn't a snake. It was too big. It could be a big snake. How big did snakes get? Taylor didn't want it to be a snake. Closer. Taylor's eyes strained to see in the dark. Then it touched her bare arm. She flung out her hand and felt hair. Not a snake. Then what?

Taylor didn't want to scream again, but she had no choice. This scream wasn't as loud as the last one.

The thing jumped off the bed with a soft hard thud.

"Wassa matter?" Nicole turned on her bedside light and sat up. "Oh, it's you again." Her eyes were half closed against the light. This time she looked crabby.

"Something was on my bed," Taylor whispered.

"What?"

"I don't know. It moved. It sat on my stomach. I think it's under the cot."

Nicole stared at her a moment. "Maybe you were having another nightmare."

"No, I was awake."

"Maybe it was a ghost."

"No, I think it was an animal."

Nicole grinned. "It could have been a snake." She didn't look scared.

"It had fur. Snakes don't have fur."

"A hairy spider?"

"It was too big for a spider. Spiders don't thud."

"A rat maybe." She looked like she hoped it was a rat.

"That's what I thought. Do you have rats in here?"

"No, we never have rats. Panther wouldn't allow them."

"Panther?"

"Come here, Panther." A big black cat with eyes as green as Nicole's stalked out from under the cot. It jumped up beside Nicole, rubbing against her and purring loudly. "It's just my cat," she said.

"I didn't know you had a cat. Why didn't you tell me you had one? Why didn't you tell me he might jump on me?"

"He doesn't come in the house much here. Too much going on outside. I didn't know he would jump on you. He probably came to find out who was here. Are you going to scream any more tonight?"

"I hope not," Taylor said. Twice in one night was enough. She wouldn't scream again, no matter what she saw in this house. At least Dad and Sylvia hadn't heard her this time. Taylor didn't know what time it was, but they had probably gone to bed by now and couldn't hear her through the thick stone wall.

Nicole turned out the light again. Taylor closed her eyes, but sleep wouldn't come. How was she going to last through the summer?

Something was in the middle of the room. Taylor sensed it, but she didn't want to look. She squinted through her eyelashes. Something was there. A light. She turned her head toward it and opened her eyes. The room was black but in the center of the floor stood a woman in a long dress. A faint aura of greenish light surrounded her in the darkness as she wrung her hands. And then she was gone.

Was it Sylvia?

Taylor lay awake for a long time with her eyes tightly closed. She didn't want to see anybody or anything else tonight in this room.

EVERYBODY HAD A THEORY ABOUT THE FACE IN THE WINDOW.

"It was an alien," Peter said, his mouth full of cereal.

"Taylor's imagination," Sylvia said.

"A car light reflection," Dad said, pouring juice.

Nicole didn't say anything, but the look she gave Taylor was unmistakable. You were just trying to get attention, her look said. Taylor decided not to mention the woman she'd seen.

"A Martian," Peter insisted.

"Nobody lives on Mars, dodo," Nicole said. "It can't sustain life."

"Life as WE know it, heh heh heh," Peter said. "There could be aliens from other universes living there in undetectable tunnels as they hop from planet to planet. Maybe Earth is next, and Taylor saw a scout."

"Have you been reading Jules Verne again?" Dad asked.

"KP duty, kids," Sylvia said. "Everyone for himself."

They rinsed their dishes and put them in the dishwasher.

"All done?" Dad asked, putting down the newspaper.

Taylor nodded. "Come down to my office then." They went down the kitchen stairs to the cellar, where his office was on one side of the hall, Sylvia's on the other. Hers was a pleasant disorder of dried flower wreaths, fabric swatches, house and wildflower books, scissors, baskets, an herb chart, two bears sitting in little rocking chairs, a number of projects under way. Dad's was much neater, with lots of books on shelves, stacks of magazines and papers, a bust of Voltaire.

"You can e-mail your mother every morning," Dad said.

He turned on the computer and went back upstairs, leaving Taylor to communicate with her mother while he had coffee with Sylvia before starting work on his economics newsletter.

Hi, Mom, Taylor wrote, *I want to come home when you get back. I don't like it here. Please come get me as soon as you can. Love, Taylor.*

She clicked on "Send" and stared at the screen, waiting for a reply. When it didn't come, she e-mailed again and told her mother to please answer fast.

No reply. Mom was probably already busy out in New Mexico. Taylor deleted her messages so Dad wouldn't see them.

He came back with a mug of coffee. "That was quick."

"There wasn't much to say. I just got here." She remained at the computer.

"OK. I have a lot of work to do this morning. Later we can play another game of Scrabble. OK?"

Taylor shrugged. "Sure, Dad." Actually she did mind but he had to work, even if he was working at home.

He tousled her hair, messing it all up after she had combed it so carefully.

"Da-ad!" He grinned, but his eyes were already on the computer screen. Taylor went out on the back porch. She had nowhere else to go. She wasn't going to stay in Nicole's room one minute more than she had to.

Peter was in a hammock under giant trees reading his way through a stack of Tarzan books. Nicole was off somewhere. Now what? she thought. What am I supposed to do now? And for the rest of the six weeks I'm supposed to stay here if Mom doesn't come rescue me? Read until my eyes fall out?

In a bookcase in the upstairs hall Taylor found a copy of *Kon-Tiki,* about sailing on a balsa raft from Peru to the Easter Islands, and settled down to read, but her thoughts kept drifting back to her problem: a whole summer with stuck-up Nicole and a busy dad, Peter with one arm in a cast and his nose in a book.

Lunch was everybody for themselves. Peter ate his in the hammock, Dad and Sylvia in their offices. Nicole was nowhere around. Taylor made a cheese and tomato sand-wich and took it to the summerhouse to watch minnows. Green dragonflies hovered above the water. The house drowsed.

No faces stared from the attic windows today. Taylor decided she had imagined everything the day before. It was the strangeness, that was all. The house was terribly old. It had been built in 1754, Sylvia had said at supper, but the first cabin it was built around was even older, 1745. Taylor couldn't imagine things that old. Yesterday the house had seemed spooky, but that face in the window had been like Dad said, a reflection of car lights. The rat had turned out to be Panther the cat, who was just curious. And the woman? Either Sylvia or a dream. Nothing to be afraid of. She could rough it without a zillion TV channels. And even if Dad was busy, at least he was around. She could see him and talk to him every day.

Taylor threw a breadball, and the minnows raced after it. She glanced back at the attic window. A face peered through the panes. Someone was up there again, looking out the window. She blinked. The figure was gone. It had been heat waves. Or her imagination. Or Nicole.

On the other side of the house Taylor found a path through the woods between trees festooned with thick wisteria vines hung with purple flowers like bunches of grapes. Somewhere ahead she heard people noises. She couldn't understand the words. Somebody laughed. She followed the sound. Her feet were silent on the well-trodden path. The noises came from a tent of the vines so thick that she couldn't see through them. Just as she reached the tent, her foot snapped a branch. The noises stopped.

Taylor pulled aside a vine and found Nicole and a boy sitting on cushions. He must be Cody. He had dark hair, a pointed nose, brown eyes, and wore a fake brown mustache. He looked surprised but said, "Hi," then grinned. But Nicole didn't. She scrambled to her feet and advanced toward Taylor with her hands on her hips. Taylor backed up.

"What are you doing here? Spying on me! Well, go away. This is our place," she said, sticking out her chin.

"I wasn't spying on you," Taylor replied. "I didn't know who was in there. You could have been fairies or elves or gnomes," she added half jokingly, half sarcastically.

If she had expected Nicole to find it funny, she was wrong. Nicole scowled fiercely. "I may have to share my room with you, but I don't have to share my secret places or my friends. Now go away."

The boy stopped grinning and stared at Taylor. Their faces were a stone wall. Taylor let the vines fall back. She ran down the path but soon realized she had taken a wrong turn. The woods were deeply overgrown with other vines that clambered up trees, some with stems so thick that she could see why Peter had tried to swing on them. She reached up and grabbed a lush one with ivylike leaves and swung her weight on it. The vine held, but she didn't try the Tarzan thing. She didn't want to break her arm, too.

Taylor couldn't forget the look on Nicole's face. Why did Nicole hate her? She had never done anything to Nicole. It was the other way around. She should be the one who got to do the hating, not Nicole. Nicole got to live with her dad all the year round, and Taylor only got to see him in summer and he was busy working then. It wasn't fair.

By the time Taylor reached the house she had worked herself into a good case of hating Nicole back. And she was mad at her dad, too. But then he came out and played Scrabble with her and Peter the rest of the afternoon and that made things better.

CHAPTER

5

TAYLOR DECIDED NOT TO SPEAK TO NICOLE AGAIN. AT supper she picked silently at her tuna casserole. Nicole ignored her, chatting about July Daze with her mother and Steve.

"I'm thinking about writing a little history of the house," Sylvia said. "There's so much history in this area. I have the eighteenth-century history of this house, but I'm sure there is a lot of it from the Civil War period. I would like to include that, but there's not much time. Maybe you kids can help me with it."

Nicole concentrated on her peas. Peter ducked his head and mumbled something. Taylor didn't say anything. She didn't think she was included.

But Dad did. "That's a great idea. Taylor likes to write. She can help."

Taylor kept quiet. Nicole glowered and stabbed a carrot with her fork.

"Oh, that would be wonderful, Taylor," Sylvia said. "I'd really appreciate it."

At Dad's look, Taylor said she would be glad to do it. Nicole shot her a look of green hate from under her lashes and stabbed her peas.

After supper Nicole asked if they could play outside.

"Yes, but stay in the yard," Sylvia said.

"Come on." Nicole headed out the door with Peter behind her. Taylor hesitated. Did Nicole mean her, too?

"Hey, Taylor, come on," Peter called over his shoulder, so Taylor tagged along to see what was going to happen. Maybe Nicole was sorry for the way she acted earlier.

The boy from the secret place was waiting outside.

"This is Cody," Nicole said to the air behind Taylor.

"Hi." He lifted a hand and grinned like nothing had happened earlier. Without the mustache, he looked a little like Billy Brown from her class at school.

"Hi," Taylor said.

"Let's play hide-and-seek," Peter suggested.

Taylor waited for Nicole to sneer and say that was a baby game.

"OK," Nicole said to her surprise. "One dinosaur, two . . ." Nicole had to be different, even at counting out. "The dinosaur gets you." Taylor was it. She sat on the front steps with her eyes closed and counted to one hundred. It took forever to find them. They knew all the hiding places, while she had to guess at them. She heard a lot of giggling in the

shadows, and once Panther stalked from under the screened porch. Peter was behind a bush near the front steps where she thought nobody would hide. Cody was behind the barn. By the time she caught everybody but Nicole, it was too late to start another game. They called Nicole in and sat on the edge of the front steps watching fireflies in the trees. Lightning bugs, Cody called them.

"Nicole said you saw a ghost last night," he said to Taylor.

"It was probably a car light."

"Was it round?"

Taylor nodded.

"Did it have craters that made a face like in the moon?"

How did he know? "Yes, that's exactly what it looked like."

"That wasn't a car light. It was a ghost." His voice dwindled to a whisper.

The warm June night suddenly felt cooler to Taylor.

"How do you know?" she asked.

"Everybody knows around here. It was Abel Swain's ghost. He's the man who built the house. He was hit by a train and his head was cut off. The head comes back looking for the rest of him. It can't get inside without his body. When it finds his body, then the ghost will come in." He sounded pleased at the prospect.

A chill ran down Taylor's spine.

"I never heard that," Peter said.

"I did," Nicole said. "I heard it. But I never saw it."

"Only certain people can see ghosts," Cody said.

"What kind of people?" Taylor almost squeaked.

"Their next victims," he said in a piercing whisper, his eyes wide and staring in the light from the house windows.

"Aw, I don't believe that stuff," Peter said.

"I'm glad I never saw it," Nicole said quickly.

Insects screeched in the dark around them. An owl hooted somewhere in the woods. Taylor felt that anything could happen in this spooky place. Suddenly the phone rang inside, and the spell was broken.

A minute later Sylvia said from the door, "It's late. Time to roost, chickens. That was your mom, Cody. Can you see your way home?"

"I have my flashlight," Cody said. "Anyway, I could follow that path with my eyes closed."

Nicole took the first shower again. Taylor felt itchy as she waited, scratching her arms, her left ankle, all of her fingers. In the shower she discovered little beads of clear liquid popping out all over her. Was it the plague? The curse of Abel Swain?

"Poison ivy," Sylvia said when Taylor showed the blisters to her. She gave Taylor some lotion to put on them. It helped a little but didn't stop most of the itching.

Taylor was so engrossed in her scratching that she forgot to think about the head of Abel Swain. Not until she was lying in the cot with the lights off. She wouldn't look out the window. If she didn't see it, it didn't exist. She kept her eyes

tightly shut as she scratched. But she couldn't help wondering if it was there. Scratch, scratch.

Maybe if she ignored it, it would go away.

What was she thinking? Of course it wasn't there. Ghosts don't exist. Abel Swain probably died peacefully in bed, head still firmly attached to the rest of him. But what if he didn't? What if his head was out there? What if his body was somewhere in the house? In this room? What if his head suddenly swung into the window and connected with his body? What if he then turned her into a ghost?

Taylor opened her eyes.

Abel Swain's face—white, ghostly, and craterous—loomed just outside the window. It was staring straight at Taylor.

CHAPTER

6

TAYLOR YELPED AND TRIED TO JUMP OUT OF THE COT. IT collapsed into a heap with her in the middle. She thought Abel Swain was holding her down as she fought to get clear of the bedcovers. "Help," she cried, rolling onto the floor.

Lights came on in the hall. Footsteps hurried to the door. It opened. Dad and Sylvia and Peter came in.

"What's happening in here?" Dad asked.

Nicole turned on her light. "Whazzat?" she said in a sleepy voice, but her eyes were bright with glee.

"I saw it," Taylor said. "The face. It was staring in the window at me, about to come in. I tried to get out of bed and something wouldn't let me."

Taylor untangled herself from the wreck of the cot as Dad examined it. "The cot collapsed because the right leg broke. I'll see about repairing it tomorrow."

"Meanwhile you'll have to share Nicole's bed, Taylor," Sylvia said.

Nicole gave Taylor a fierce look but didn't say anything as she moved over to the side by the lamp.

Taylor didn't want to sleep with Nicole any more than Nicole wanted her to. She got in on the other side and stayed as close to the edge as she could.

Peter danced around, jabbing the air with his cast. "Where's the ghost! I want to see the ghost."

"All right, everybody settle down now," Dad said. "Let's get some sleep."

"Peter, go back to bed," Sylvia said.

"Awww. They get to have all the fun."

The lights were out and the house was quiet again. Nicole was soon breathing deeply. Asleep already? Taylor scratched the itch on her left hand and kept her eyes open, watching for the face. But the window remained black.

Something was in the room. Taylor glimpsed movement.

The woman glided into the center of the room. Taylor lay paralyzed, watching. It wasn't Sylvia. This woman wore a long dress with a bustle on the back. She seemed to glow with a greenish light around her. She wrung her hands in anguish as she paced the room, touching things that Taylor couldn't see, things that maybe were no longer there. Her ghostly hands mimed opening cupboards, pulling out drawers.

Taylor put her hand over her mouth. She wouldn't scream again or yell. She wouldn't even whimper. Please go away, she whispered silently to the woman, afraid to close her eyes.

The woman dissolved. There was no doubt left in Taylor's mind: the woman was a ghost. But whose? Not Abel Swain's. Taylor lay rigid until the room began to lighten before dawn, and then she slept.

"The cot is a dead loss," Dad said upon closer examination the next morning.

Taylor felt uncomfortable about breaking the cot, even though it was old.

"You two will have to share Nicole's bed," Sylvia said.

Nicole's eyes narrowed in fury. It's all your fault, she seemed to say on her way to the wisteria tent to meet Cody.

Taylor was miserable. Mom had e-mailed that she should be thrilled to spend her summer in a house like Swain's Fancy, that Taylor had always loved old houses, all that history, a part of America, she should make it her summer project to find out all she could about it, she was a lucky girl, etc., etc.

Peter offered her his Tarzan books, and she read for a while in a chair beside him in the hammock, but she was too miserable to concentrate and couldn't stop her thoughts from straying to the story of Abel Swain.

"Peter, why is the house called Swain's Fancy?"

"Dunno." He turned a page without looking up.

Taylor decided to ask Dad. Maybe he would know. She went in the house and down the cellar stairs to his office. He wasn't there, but Sylvia was in hers.

"Sylvia, why is this house called Swain's Fancy?"

She was on her computer, a pencil stuck in her hair, fabric swatches dangling from her mouth as her fingers flew over the keys. She said something that sounded like, "Deadline. Swain preffed thisslund. Fancied it."

Taylor knew what "deadline" meant. Sylvia's column had to be in by a certain time for it to go to the printer. She went back upstairs, ate a banana from the fruit bowl in the dining room, and mulled over Sylvia's words. Preffed? Thisslund? Fancied? Finally she decided that Abel Swain must have preferred this piece of land. He fancied it. That must be what "fancy" meant then instead of what it usually means now, which is "decorated."

She went out on the front porch and looked at the carving over the door, SWAIN'S FANCY 1754. Poor Abel. Getting his head cut off by a train. If that was what really happened to him.

Dad drove up in his Jeep. "Hi, Taylor. I had to go to the post office. What are you doing out here by yourself?"

"Peter's reading in the hammock. Nicole is off with Cody. Sylvia's on deadline."

"Hmmm. Like that, is it?"

Taylor nodded. Dad seemed to understand about Nicole.

"Dad, did Abel Swain really get his head cut off by a train?"

"No, of course not. Why did you think that?"

"Cody said he did."

"Cody's wrong. Look at the date over the door. What does it say?"

"Swain's Fancy 1754."

"And when were trains invented?"

"I don't know. Sometime in the 1800s."

"I'll give you a clue. The first railroads in this country ran in 1828 in Baltimore. So what Cody said couldn't be true."

"Why not?"

"You tell me."

Taylor thought for a minute. "The house was built years before the railroad. Abel Swain would probably have been at least twenty years old in 1754 when he built the house, maybe even older. He would have been at least ninety-four when the first railroad ran. So why couldn't he have had his head cut off?"

Dad smiled. "Good thinking. But there was no railroad around here for a long time. Swain was at least twenty when he came here in 1745 and built the cabin that he lived in until he built this house."

"If he was born in 1725, he could have lived to be a hundred and three," Taylor said, "and taken a ride on the first railroad, fallen out, and got his head cut off."

Dad laughed. "Yes, it's possible. But Swain already had a wife and children when he came here. I think he was older than twenty. It's more likely that Cody was telling a tale."

He went into the house, leaving Taylor to think about Abel Swain and Cody's story and why he had told it to her.

Nicole and Cody wouldn't let her join them in their day games. Why had they let her play last night?

Then she thought of another question. Why hadn't Nicole ever seen the face? Something was going on and she bet Nicole was behind it. She'd been excited, not scared the first time the face had appeared. That wasn't normal. She should have been scared, too.

Taylor decided to look for clues. She started with Nicole's room, being careful not to muss the clothes folded in drawers or to leave anything out of place. Everything seemed to be just what it should be. She checked under the bed and found dust bunnies, dental floss, a box of old clothes, bits of dance costumes, wigs, a pair of wings. Taylor thought it would be fun to put on plays with these. But she shoved the box back under the bed and blew the dust bunnies with it. She left the dental floss, too. She wasn't going to clean up Nicole's mess.

The stairs to the attic were in the hall behind a door that creaked as she opened it. Taylor ignored the noise and went up. The fifth step was odd, steeper than the others. Sylvia hadn't had time to tackle the attic. It was musty, dusty, cobwebby, just the kind of attic Taylor liked. Some boxes had not yet been unpacked from the move, but some of the older dusty boxes and things had probably been left in the house by people who had lived here before. She found a stack of *Life* magazines from the 1940s and '50s in a pile on the floor. Boxes, leftover debris from workmen, a broken vase, some boxes labeled in Sylvia's hand were stacked near the window on the end. More cobwebs. Taylor reached out to break a long line of cobweb. But the web held. She looked down at the end of it in her hand. It was as strong as dental floss. She pulled on it.

It *was* dental floss. She followed it to a window at the front of the house, and there on the floor a face—white, ghostly, and craterous—stared up at her.

Dusty footprints surrounded the face, which appeared now to be cardboard painted with some kind of luminous paint.

Nicole!

She was responsible for nearly scaring Taylor to death. But how had she managed to make the face float outside the window when she was in bed the whole time?

The attic window was just above the one where Taylor had slept in the cot. Nicole must have come up here and dropped the face out the window, then run the floss downstairs to her bed. It wouldn't have been noticeable on the floor at night or any other time unless somebody was looking under the bed. She probably tied the end to her bedpost and gave it slack to make the face appear and pulled it taut to make it disappear. When people came into the room, she made it disappear, then pulled it up into the attic in the morning where nobody could see it. That was why she didn't want Taylor in her bed. Her movements would have jiggled the bed, and Taylor would have known she was doing it.

Taylor had to admit it was a clever trick. But why did Nicole hate her so much that she would play a mean trick like that? What had she ever done to Nicole?

She picked up the face and went downstairs to find Nicole and have it out with her.

As Taylor neared the wisteria tent, she decided to give Nicole a scare. Stepping carefully to avoid making noise, she approached the tent. She threw the end of the dental floss over a limb and lowered the face through a slot in the vines.

"Wooooooooooo! Wooooooooooo!" She made a high scary noise, the kind she thought a ghost would make. "Eeeeeeeeee!"

"Aarrrrgh!"

"Yeooooow!"

"What's that?"

Nicole and Cody jumped out of the vine tent. Their faces wore scared looks. Taylor laughed.

"What do you think you're doing?" Nicole demanded.

"Just returning Abel's head to you," Taylor said.

Nicole glared at her but for once was speechless.

"I know it was you doing those things," Taylor said.

Nicole and Cody looked at her, then broke into laughter. "You were so funny! Your face was as white as Abel Swain's!" Nicole said between giggles.

It hadn't been funny to Taylor. She was furious, but she didn't want them to know. "It really was childish. If I'd known you were into such baby stuff, I would have guessed it was you earlier. I know how you did the face, but how did you do the woman?"

Nicole stopped laughing. "What woman?"

"The one that comes after Abel. Probably his wife. Or girl-friend. She's probably looking for his head!"

"There's no woman. You're making that up." Nicole scowled.

"No, I'm not." But Nicole refused to listen. She and Cody ran off into the woods. To another of their secret places, probably. She didn't like getting caught at her tricks. But Taylor would be on guard now. They would have a hard time tricking her again.

CHAPTER

7

"WILL YOU STOP THAT SCRATCHING?" NICOLE SNAPPED AS SHE turned the page of her book.

"I can't. It itches too much." Taylor looked up from the letter she was writing to her best friend, Annette, at home. Annette was going to the beach with both of her parents for summer vacation. She wasn't stuck in an old house with a stepsister who hated her. Lucky Annette. Taylor wrote about Nicole and her mean tricks.

"Put something on it. Didn't Mom give you something?"

"I'm covered with the stuff, but it only helps for about a nanosecond."

"I can't stand all that scratching." Nicole got out of bed and went to talk to her mother. Sylvia came back with her.

Taylor scratched vigorously.

"Taylor, don't scratch so much," Sylvia said. "You'll make it worse."

"I have to! It itches. It couldn't be any worse than it is."

"All right, Nicole. I can see your point. Taylor, you can sleep in the other bedroom."

Sylvia took sheets out of a chest in the other bedroom, and Taylor helped her make up the bed. Dad brought in a lamp and plugged it in. "It's not in period but I know you'll want to read before you go to sleep."

"Thanks, Dad."

He and Sylvia went downstairs. Taylor was alone in the museum room. The antique bed was high off the floor, with four tall posts that soared above her. A tall chest stood against one wall, another with drawers against the wall opposite, and a trunk and a rocking chair on the wall between them. A dark painting of fruit hung over the chest with drawers. The room was gloomy and plain despite the bowl of fragrant potpourri on the stand beside the bed. Taylor was glad she hadn't lived in those days. She liked her own cheerful poppy-red, grass-green, and pear-yellow room at home in Washington, her instant communication with the computer, her little TV, her rows of books in the shelves, her collection of stuffed animals. But this room was better than sleeping in a bed with someone who hated her. Nicole couldn't try to scare Taylor now.

She settled back on the pillows and opened her book, *The Once and Future King*. Taylor read a long time, losing herself in the adventures of a boy called Wart. It helped her forget the itching.

Suddenly the door opened and Nicole rushed in, breathless and scared-looking. "Can I sleep in here?"

"No." Taylor didn't have to think twice about her reply. What was she scheming about now? "You had me moved out of your room. Do you want this one, too?"

"Please. Look, I know it was a dirty trick about Abel and the head." Nicole stopped and gulped. "I'm sorry. Really sorry. I'll make it up to you. Please let me sleep here."

"No. This is just another one of your tricks."

"It's not. I swear it's not. Cross my heart." Nicole crossed her heart.

Taylor was sure Nicole was capable of crossing her heart and then doing any kind of dirty trick. But she did seem scared. "Why should I let you? You don't want me here. You've made that plain. Well, I don't want you in the room with me either. So go away."

But Nicole wouldn't go. "I don't blame you for feeling that way. It was mean. I won't do it anymore. Please."

"No."

"I'll be nice from now on. I promise."

Taylor didn't answer.

"Cross my heart?"

"No."

"I'll put it in writing." She grabbed Taylor's box of stationery and pen and scribbled furiously. "Here. This proves I'll be nice."

Taylor read the note twice, searching for tricks. "I'm sorry I tried to scare Taylor with the Abel Swain ghost head & I promise not to do it again & to be nice. Signed: Nicole Elizabeth Thorson."

"OK, you can stay. Just for tonight. But if it's another one of your tricks, I'm telling."

"It's not. Really, it's not. And if it is, you can show the note to Mom, and I'll get in trouble."

It would be interesting to see how she would play a trick in here. Taylor would be on alert to catch her.

Nicole got in bed, and Taylor turned off the light. "Why do you want to sleep in here?" she asked in the dark.

"I don't want to talk about it," Nicole said.

Taylor kept her eyes open, straining to see whatever was going to happen in the dark room, to be ready for Nicole's trick, whatever it was. Nicole was quiet, but it didn't sound like she was asleep. How long would she wait?

Years seemed to pass.

Taylor's eyes grew heavy. It was hard to keep them open. Maybe Nicole wasn't going to try anything. Maybe she could forget about tricks and just go to sleep.

The room grew lighter. Taylor's eyes sprang open. It couldn't be morning already. She hadn't been asleep yet. A woman glided into the dark room. Through the door. The closed door. She stood in the center of the floor with greenish light around her, wringing her hands. Taylor lay still, gritting her teeth. She was determined not to give Nicole the satisfaction of knowing that she had seen the manufactured ghost.

Suddenly a hand gripped her arm. Taylor wanted to yell but refused to let Nicole know she was scared.

The woman took a step toward the bed. And then she faded into the darkness of the room.

Taylor lay rigid. Beside her, Nicole let out her breath. "Did you see th-that?"

"What?" It was hard to be brave, but she couldn't let Nicole get the best of her again.

"Th-that woman."

"No, I didn't see any woman. Where was she?"

"Th-there. In the middle of the room."

This had gone on long enough. Taylor turned on the lamp. "I don't know how you did it. You didn't know I was going to be sleeping in here. Or did you?"

Nicole looked terrified. Her teeth were still chattering. "Wh-what are you talking about?"

This was too much. Nobody's teeth chattered like that. "Maybe you planned to tell Sylvia I made too much noise. You knew she would move me in here so you set the whole trick up ahead of time just in case. How did you do it?"

"I didn't do anything." Nicole gained control of her teeth.

"That's a nice touch—the chattering teeth. But you can't fool me."

"It wasn't a trick. Look, I admitted Cody and I rigged up the face. But we had nothing to do with this. Honest."

Taylor didn't entirely believe her. Nicole was a good actor. "Then if she isn't a trick, who is she?"

"I don't want to say it."

"Well?" Taylor waited.

"We can talk about it in daylight. I don't want to go to sleep in a haunt—in here."

"We could go back to your room."

"No. I saw her in there, too."

"Me, too," Taylor said.

Nicole's surprise was genuine. "You saw her in there?"

"Both nights. I was scared. I thought she was one of your tricks. I don't think she'll come back," Taylor said. "She didn't before."

"She came in here after I saw her in my room," Nicole said.

"I only saw her once each night. Maybe she won't come back. She didn't the other times." Taylor turned off the light. She planned to stay awake all night. Her eyes closed.

The room was as cold as a refrigerator. Arctic wind blew over her, but where was it coming from? She tried to pull the covers up but only had a sheet. The wind blew harder. She was freezing, but she refused to open her eyes. And then the air settled back into normal June temperature.

CHAPTER

8

NICOLE ACTED AS IF NOTHING HAD HAPPENED THE NIGHT before, that she hadn't begged to spend the night in Taylor's room, that they hadn't seen a ghost together. She poured milk over her cereal, ignoring Taylor. When Taylor suggested a game of Monopoly, she looked at the refrigerator behind Taylor's head and said, "Only babies play games like that."

Taylor had thought she would be different today. She was the same old stuck-up Nicole. She didn't want to be friends with Taylor. Or sisters.

Dad was busy in his office, Sylvia in hers. Taylor sighed as she thought about the long day with nothing to do. She sent her mother an e-mail without mentioning her problems with Nicole or what happened last night. She just told her about sleeping in a bedroom with furniture from the eighteenth century. *I'm glad I live in this century,* she typed. Mom couldn't do anything while she was in New Mexico. She would just say they had to work it out themselves, that they were going to be stepsisters forever, so the sooner, the better.

The day dragged by. Taylor recolored a big magenta T over the C in Nicole's name on Peter's cast. He didn't even stop reading to watch. Now all the letters in Taylor's name were there, even if they were intersected by Nicole's. Peter offered her another Tarzan book, but she felt restless. She wanted to do something active. She wandered out to the summerhouse and stared at minnows in the pond. A frog croaked happily somewhere. A tiny breeze rippled the water, and for an instant she felt a kind of urgency—but for what?

Taylor sat on the edge of the bridge and dabbled her toes in the pond water, sending the minnows darting. She looked up at the house. The face wasn't there today. Suddenly, the puzzle pieces began to fit together. The face she had seen the first day and the other time hadn't been Nicole or any other living person or a reflection or trick of the light. That face was a ghost. Maybe the same ghost that glided into the bedrooms at night, the woman with the greenish aura who seemed to be looking for something. Why was that ghost searching? And for what? These questions were more pieces of the puzzle. Taylor didn't know how to fit them together, but she knew that somehow they were important.

Peter ate lunch with her on the porch. Dad had gone to Winchester again. Sylvia had finished her column and now was concentrating on July Daze, which were getting closer.

"What do Nicole and Cody do every day?" she asked Peter as he cracked a hard-boiled egg and peeled it with one hand.

He shrugged. "I don't know. I think they make up plays or something."

"Two-people plays?"

"Guesso." He bit half the egg at once.

"Seems to me plays would be better with more people." Taylor thought of the costume pieces under Nicole's bed.

"Yeah."

"This is a long summer."

"Bummer summer." He crammed the rest of the egg in.

"Aren't there any malls or anything around?"

"No. Not unless you go to Winchester or Martinsburg."

"How far's that?"

"'Bout fifteen miles to each one." His mouth was eggy all the way around.

"There's nowhere else to go?"

"Maybe the library."

Taylor jumped up. "Let's go then." She could look for a book to use in writing about the house for Sylvia.

"You can walk if you want to," Sylvia said when they asked her. "I'm too busy to drive you right now, but I'll pick you up in a little while on my way to the store. Peter, you can help Taylor with her research on the house."

"Aw, Ma, it's at least two miles."

"Not even one. You can wait until I go or walk. I prefer

that you walk. You can use some exercise, Peter. You broke your arm, not your leg. It'll be good for you," she said.

They walked along the road, past black-and-white cows lying around under the few trees in the pastures. Closer to Burneytown, they passed houses, some of them old-looking with fancy wooden trim, though none looked as old as Swain's Fancy. They didn't see any children and Peter said he didn't know any from town except for Cody.

"You'll meet kids when you go to school," Taylor said.

"Yeah." Peter didn't seem happy about it. "They'll all be new," he said.

"Well, when you're a kid, almost everybody is new."

"Guesso."

As Taylor thought about it, she realized that although her dad was her same old dad, he was also a new stepdad to Peter and Nicole. She was the same old Taylor but a new stepsister. It was odd, like finding rooms you didn't know were there in your house.

The library was in an old wooden house with lacy trim painted slate blue, dark red, navy, and cream. The books were in different rooms, one for children's books, one for adults, another for nonfiction books. All of the books looked old. Taylor found some Jeeves and Wooster books. Peter picked a pile of paperback Zane Grey westerns.

"Do you have any books on the history of Burneytown?" Taylor asked Mrs. Mills, the librarian, a short lady with curly gray hair.

"Not on the town itself. But we do have one about the county," she said. She went to the nonfiction room and brought back a thick old book that she handed to Taylor. "Is this what you are looking for?"

Taylor read the title. *The History of Warfield County*. It didn't look like anybody had checked it out in a long time. Probably one of those dry, boring history books. But she had asked for it, so she took it. Mrs. Mills checked it out on Peter's card.

"Are you interested in history?" she asked Taylor.

Taylor nodded and explained about the project for July Daze.

"This whole area in the Eastern Panhandle was constantly in turmoil during the Civil War," Mrs. Mills said. "Martinsburg, West Virginia, changed hands between Union and Confederate army control ten times and Winchester, Virginia, seventy-six times!"

"Wow!" Peter said.

"Why did they go back and forth so much?" Taylor asked.

"The Union needed the railhead in Martinsburg. It was the gateway to the Shenandoah Valley with all its farm produce, and also the gateway to the coal mines in the rest of what is now West Virginia. And they needed it for troop movements into the Valley. Mr. Lincoln refused to let the Confederacy hold on to this part of the state."

She sounded like she knew the president personally.

Mrs. Mills was just warming to her subject. "The Confederates weren't able to hold the area long, so they tore up rail lines and set fire to the equipment when they had to retreat. They dragged locomotives south, deep into the Shenandoah Valley from Martinsburg to Strasburg, Virginia, a distance of about fifty miles!

"Colonel John Mosby's Rangers raided the Panhandle when it was under Union control. Mosby himself was called the Gray Ghost because he could slip in and out right under the Union army's nose. He once spent the night at my great-grandfather's house."

Taylor thought Mrs. Mills would have talked all night if Sylvia hadn't come to pick them up. She drove to the grocery in Burneytown, and they helped her fill a cart and carry the bags to the car. They persuaded her to cook fried chicken and potato salad for supper, but they had to promise to peel the potatoes and eggs.

"Deal!" Peter said. "I'll crack the eggs and Taylor can peel them."

"No fair," Taylor said.

Peter cradled his arm in the sling. "You wouldn't make a wounded boy work, would you?"

Taylor laughed. "You weren't having any trouble at lunch. I'll do the potatoes, you peel the eggs."

Nicole had to play with Taylor and Peter after supper if she wanted to play outside the house. Taylor was one of the group now that she knew Cody and was friends with Peter. The game was again hide-and-seek, but this time Peter insisted on counting out and Nicole was it first. Taylor flattened herself behind some ferns near the woods, hidden unless somebody tripped over her. She sneaked back into base. Cody got caught and had to be it. This was more fun than the rigged game the night before. This was the way the game was supposed to be played.

At bedtime Taylor slathered herself in the new itch cream Sylvia had gotten for her and went alone to the antique room. Nicole had been believable the night before when she begged to come in Taylor's room, but now Taylor was beginning to have doubts. Maybe Nicole had staged the whole thing the way she staged Abel Swain's head and the plays she and Cody put on. Maybe it was part of a complicated plan that would be revealed tonight. What would she do next? Taylor didn't trust Nicole's promise of no more tricks.

When Taylor was ready for bed, the door to the hall slowly opened. "Taylor, can I sleep in here?" Nicole whispered.

What nerve. "No."

Nicole looked surprised. "Why not? You let me last night."

"You can't sleep in here at night and ignore me all day."

"Why not?"

"Because I won't let you, that's why not. Now go back to your room before I call Dad and show him the note."

"You think he'll side with you. You think you're so smart. Daddy's little girl."

Taylor lifted her chin. "Yes, I'm Daddy's little girl and

Daddy's big girl, too. Just because you get to have him all the time doesn't change anything with him and me. So go back to your room, you stuck-up snob."

"Baby!" Nicole stuck her tongue out.

"I'm not the baby," Taylor said, but Nicole slammed the door to have the final word in the argument.

Taylor got into bed and opened her book. She was seething. Who did Nicole think she was anyway?

The house settled down, quiet except for the noise of crickets and frogs outside. Taylor soon forgot her anger as she read about the antics of Jeeves and Wooster. Then out of the corner of her eye, she saw the door slowly open.

It was Nicole again.

"I'm sorry," she said. "You're not a baby. I get mad sometimes because you have a dad and get to see him and I don't."

"What do you mean you don't?"

"I don't get to see my dad."

"Not ever?"

"Not for a year. He's in Pakistan or somewhere like that. He's always traveling. That's why he and Mom got divorced. He was always gone, and she wanted him to stay home. He sends us a postcard every now and then."

Nicole looked so miserable that Taylor felt sorry for her. Taylor was also on guard. Nicole could be acting a part. She would check with Peter tomorrow. A year was a long time. She'd only seen her dad twice since Christmas, twice in six months, but compared to Nicole that was a lot.

"I don't know why you want to sleep in here. You didn't want me in your room," Taylor said.

Nicole whispered something.

"What?"

"I saw her again."

"Who?"

"You know. Her. Just now."

"She'll probably come in here next like she did before. She won't hurt you. She doesn't do anything but wring her hands and look in furniture that's not here anymore."

"I know. But it's scarier when I'm alone."

That was true. Even if she didn't like Nicole, Taylor didn't want to face the woman alone either. "OK. Just for tonight."

Nicole got in bed and closed her eyes. Taylor went back to her book. She laughed aloud at Muriel and Bertie.

"What's so funny?" Nicole asked. She read the title of the book. "Oh, Jeeves and Wooster. I've seen them on TV. I didn't know they were in a book."

"Lots of books."

"Why did you call me a snob?"

"Because you don't ever play with me."

"You don't seem to like me either," Nicole said.

"You didn't like me first. And I was mad because you get to see my dad all the time, and I had only seen him a little since he bought this house."

"Steve's nice. You're lucky he's your dad. I wish he were my dad."

"He's my dad but he's your stepdad, and you get to live with him. That's the next best thing," Taylor said. And she realized it was. It must be awful for Nicole and Peter not to see their dad. "We can share him," she added. "And Jeeves and Wooster." She handed Nicole another of the Wodehouse books.

They read until Taylor's eyes began to droop. "Ready to turn out the light?"

"OK."

She turned the switch, and the room was instantly black. Taylor closed her eyes, but in a few minutes she knew that someone else was in the room, someone besides Nicole. Against her will she opened her eyes and saw the woman with the bustle standing as before in the middle of the room. This time she didn't disappear quickly. She walked around as she had in Nicole's room, searching, her hands opening cupboards that weren't there, opening drawers that only she could see.

Beside her, Nicole was rigid also, watching.

The woman glided toward the bed. She didn't know it was there. She was going to walk through it. Taylor dived over the side, with Nicole right behind her. They hit the floor with a thump.

From under the bed they could see the bottom of the ghost's skirt. It reached the bed. And then it stopped.

CHAPTER

9

THE WOMAN TURNED AROUND AND GLIDED OUT OF THE ROOM, passing through the closed door.

"D-did you s-see that?" Nicole said.

Taylor couldn't speak. "Uh-huh," she said through tightly pressed lips.

They jumped back into bed. Taylor reached for the light.

"No, don't turn it on," Nicole said. "We're safe now. She won't come back."

"Who is she?"

"You know."

"Who?"

"I mean you know what. We both know what. I don't want to say it."

A ghost. The lady was a ghost, but neither Taylor nor Nicole would say it. They lay in the dark, unwilling to discuss what they had seen.

The room grew cold. What strange weather, Taylor thought as she drifted off to sleep.

The next morning Nicole didn't run away to the woods with Cody. After breakfast and chores, she told Taylor and Peter to come with her. Cody was waiting in the wisteria tent. They sat around on old plastic-covered pillows.

"Taylor and I have something to tell you," she said.

The others waited.

"You tell them, Taylor," she said.

"You can do it," Taylor said. It seemed silly in the daylight.

"What? Tell us what?" Peter said.

"Our house is haunted."

"Oh come on." Peter laughed.

Cody didn't. "What did you see?" he asked, his eyes excited.

Taylor and Nicole took turns telling what they had seen.

"I want to see her," Cody said. "I've never seen a ghost."

"You mean you believe in that stuff?" Peter said.

"Sure. Lots of old houses around here have ghosts. My cousin Eric saw Mosby's Rangers once, galloping across a field. Most of them are from the Civil War period. The Union and Confederate armies were all over the place in the Shenandoah Valley. And they left lots of ghosts behind after skirmishes and battles. The way they fought war then was to march shoulder-to-shoulder straight toward the enemy. They got mowed down a lot."

"I wouldn't have done that," Peter said.

"Yes you would. The armies were made up of companies of men from the same places. A lot of them were kin. If you didn't march with them you would be called a coward and nobody would ever have anything to do with you again."

"If you're dead, they won't have anything to do with you either," Peter pointed out.

"That's true. But at least you would have died bravely and your family could be proud of you."

"Still sounds dumb to me," Peter said. "But I want to see a ghost, too."

"If there is such a thing," Cody said.

"This one's real," Taylor assured him.

They made plans. Nobody suggested telling the grown-ups. This is our ghost, Taylor thought. We'll deal with it just like Mom deals with problems for Senator McKenna.

Peter asked Sylvia if Cody could spend the night. She said yes, and Cody's mom said he could.

Cody came over in time for supper. Dad made his specialty, crab cakes. It had been a long time since Taylor had had them. Dad made the best crab cakes in the world. The cakes reminded Taylor of the days when they were a family, Dad, Mom, and her. Now they were a new and bigger family that included Sylvia and Nicole and Peter.

"What are your plans tonight?" Dad asked as they ate ice cream with chocolate sauce.

"Going on a ghost hunt," Peter said.

Why was he giving away their secret? Taylor, Nicole, and Cody stopped eating and looked at the grown-ups. Peter laughed. Then Sylvia laughed and said, "Oh, you kids and your imaginations."

Going on a ghost hunt sounded exciting, like going on a treasure hunt, not scary like having a ghost glide into your room while you were trying to sleep and doing things you didn't understand and then trying to walk through your bed.

They played Clue in Peter's room until Sylvia called up the stairs, "Lights out, all."

Nicole and Taylor each went to their rooms. Taylor waited about ten seconds. Then she opened the door to the hall and met Peter and Cody. Nicole was waiting for them in her room. "Where should we sit?" Cody asked.

"Between the windows," Nicole said. "She never goes over there."

"I wouldn't want a ghost to step on me," Peter joked.

"Me neither," Cody said, but he wasn't joking.

They sat in a row against the wall, and Nicole turned off the light.

Time passed. The house settled down with its creaks and groans. Crickets screamed outside and frogs thrummed in the dark.

"How long do we have to wait?" Peter asked.

"Until she comes," Nicole said.

Taylor scratched her poison ivy. She had forgotten to use the itch cream.

"Is this supposed to be a joke?" Peter asked after awhile.

"No," Taylor and Nicole said together.

"We both saw it. Her," Taylor said. "She wears a bustled skirt like women from the late nineteenth century, and she opens drawers and things that we can't see."

"She'll come," Nicole said. "Just wait a little longer."

"This floor is hard," Peter complained.

Nicole got a folded quilt for them to sit on.

The boys complained some more. They seemed to enjoy it. Suddenly Peter gulped in mid-sentence. "I see her," he said in a strangled voice.

The woman appeared suddenly in the middle of the room, her black dress pulled back over a bustle. She wrung her hands in anguish as she glided around the room, opening ghost drawers and cupboards. Then she disappeared.

Nicole sprang for the light. The boys sat staring at the spot where the ghost had been. Peter's mouth was open. Cody looked like he wanted to go home.

Taylor got up. "Come on, let's go in the other room. She'll be in there in a few minutes. We can see her again."

"I don't know if I want to," Peter said.

"Me neither," Cody said.

"You wanted to go on a ghost hunt. Didn't you expect to find one?" Nicole asked.

"Not really," Cody said as Peter shook his head. "Eric said he would show me the ghosts but nothing ever happened. I think he made the whole thing up."

"We thought you were going to play a trick on us. Like with the face," Peter grinned. "Cody told me about it."

"It's not a trick," Nicole said. "Come on."

Taylor led the way to the antique bedroom. The boys followed reluctantly. Again they sat in a row against the wall beside the bed. Taylor leaned against the nightstand. "There must have been a bed here in her day, too," she said. "She doesn't try to walk through this one."

"That gives me the creeps," Cody said.

It was creepy, Taylor thought. But the creepiest part was why the ghost appeared, what was happening in her time to make her keep doing it over a century later. She kept her thoughts to herself.

"Watch the door," Taylor said. "She comes through it."

The room was dark. As they watched, greenish light seeped through it like mist that began to form in the shape of the woman they had seen in Nicole's room.

She walked around the room, searching in places that only she could see. As before, she came over to the bed, then turned and glided away through the closed door.

Nobody moved.

"Oh, man," Cody said.

"Jeeps," Peter said over and over.

"This happens every night?" Cody asked.

"Seems to," Taylor answered.

"Is it over?" Peter asked. "Are any more coming?"

"No," Nicole said. "That's it. Show's over."

"She only comes to these two rooms?" Cody asked. "Nowhere else in the house?"

"Nobody has seen her anywhere else," Nicole said.

Taylor didn't mention the attic. Nobody was going up there tonight.

"What do you suppose she's looking for?" Peter said.

"No telling. She seems to be looking in furniture that isn't here anymore," Nicole said.

"Let's go back to my room," Peter said.

"Somebody turn on a light," Cody said.

"Why is it so cool in here all of a sudden?" Peter asked. "It feels like somebody turned on the air-conditioning."

"We don't have air-conditioning," Nicole said.

Taylor stood up to reach the lamp beside the bed. The room swirled with an icy coldness that almost paralyzed her. She tried to reach for the switch but her hands wouldn't move. Her fingers felt frozen. The cold seemed to come from the center of the room, where blue-white pixels spun in a whirlpool of light.

Shivers ran like electricity up and down Taylor's spine as her eyes interpreted what was happening. Her mind didn't want to accept it. She stood frozen as a man materialized in front of her, a man in a uniform, his eyes blazing with a cold blue light. He stared straight at her and raised his hand.

A scream tore through the room.

CHAPTER 10

THE MAN DISAPPEARED ABRUPTLY, LEAVING A LINGERING crispness in the air.

Taylor found the lamp switch. The room jumped back into focus. "L-let's get out of here," Peter said.

They dashed to the door. Peter fumbled with the knob. Nicole wrenched it open, and they ran together to Peter's room, where they huddled on the floor beside his bed, all the lights in the room blazing.

Cody spoke first. He seemed pale under his tan. "Who screamed?"

"Not me," Peter said.

"I wanted to," Nicole said, "but I couldn't move my mouth."

"I didn't," Taylor said.

"Maybe it was him—the you know," Peter said.

"Do ghosts talk?" Taylor asked. "I mean, I thought they just did things. Without sound."

"I don't know," Nicole said. "But there are different kinds of ghosts. Like poltergeists and banshees that wail and things like that."

"I saw a book about ghosts," Taylor began.

"Where?" They all spoke at once.

"In the downstairs hall bookcase."

"What was the name of it?" Nicole asked.

"Something like *Historical Hauntings*. Let's get it."

Nobody wanted to go downstairs.

"You get it," Nicole said.

"The boys can go," Taylor said.

"No way." Peter shook his head.

"We're no braver than you are," Cody said.

"We could all go together," Taylor suggested.

"Or wait till morning," Peter said.

They decided to go down together, but Taylor insisted that they all hold hands so nobody could run off and leave anyone to face another ghost alone.

They turned on every light they could find and, hand-in-hand, went down the stairs.

Creak.

"What was that?" Cody asked.

"The stairs," Nicole said.

The stairs creaked all the way down. Taylor didn't remember so many creaks. Maybe they just sounded louder at night. They encountered no more ghosts as they retrieved the book and scampered back upstairs, where they took turns reading aloud about the different types of ghosts.

"'Basically there are three types,'" Nicole read, "'although some categories can be broken down into subcategories. The three are recording, interacting, and poltergeist.' I think our lady is a recording ghost."

"What does that mean?" Peter asked.

"She's playing a scene over and over, a scene from her life."

"That fits," Taylor said. "She does the same thing every time in the two rooms. That may be what she's doing in the attic, too."

They looked at her in horror. "She's up there, too?" Peter said.

Taylor nodded and told them about seeing her. "I was too far away to see her face clearly but I'm sure that's who it was."

"I'm never going in the attic again," Peter declared.

"I don't think she means any harm," Taylor said.

Nobody seemed to want to mention the other ghost.

"What about the other kinds of ghosts?" Cody asked.

"You mean like poltergeists?" Nicole said. "I don't think our ghosts are poltergeists. Those ghosts throw things and move things around."

"What about interacting?" Cody said.

There was a long silence.

"I don't think I want to talk about ghosts anymore tonight," Peter said.

Taylor agreed. "Yeah, daylight would be better." She stood up. Where was she going to sleep now? She wasn't ever going back to that room, not at night. Maybe not in daylight either.

"You can sleep in my room again," Nicole said.

Taylor was relieved. She would have had to sleep in the hall.

Panther was on Nicole's bed. He didn't look like a jungle panther. He looked scared. His mouth was open, and he was panting. His eyes were big and green, and his outer fur stood up in a ridge down his back. His claws were out, but he retracted them when Nicole picked him up and said, "What's the matter, Panther?"

He gradually relaxed as Taylor and Nicole climbed into bed, and he curled up between them. Soon he made a sound somewhere between purring and snoring.

"It was Panther that screamed," Taylor whispered.

"I know."

Taylor waited for Nicole to turn off the bedside lamp but she left it on, and that was OK with Taylor.

CHAPTER

11

THE WEATHER WAS GLOOMY THE NEXT MORNING. GONE WAS
the sunshine that made every day seem like a picture of
summer. Gray clouds hung heavily over the house. It
seemed to Taylor that the weather reflected the scariness of
the night before. She wished it were sunny. Somehow talking
about ghosts didn't seem as spooky when the sun lit up the
world, fluffy white clouds floated lazily overhead, butterflies
flitted from flower to flower, and birds chirped cheerfully in
the trees.

They sat on the screened porch—Cody and Peter on the
floor, Nicole draped over a cushioned wicker chair, Taylor in
a wooden rocker.

"I think the man ghost is an interactive one," Nicole said.
She didn't look happy about it.

"What do you mean?" Peter asked. "He didn't do anything."

"Well, the lady only looks for something but the man seemed, well, he—" She gulped.

"She means he seemed to be trying to s-scare us," Taylor said.

"He sure succeeded," Cody said.

"We don't know that for sure," Taylor said. She didn't want to have an interactive ghost around the house. Or anywhere in the neighborhood. Or anywhere in the state of West Virginia. "Maybe he's reenacting something and just looks like he's going to . . ." She didn't know what the ghost had been about to do. She didn't think she wanted to know why he had looked straight into her eyes.

"He looked to me like he hadn't finished something. . . ." Nicole's sentence trailed off.

They digested this unappetizing thought in silence.

Cody had been reading ahead in the book. "If we don't find out why he's haunting, and stop him, he might, well, do something really awful."

Like what? The words hung in the air, but nobody wanted to say them.

"Maybe he did something really awful in real life," Taylor said.

"He looked like he could have. He looked like a real bad guy," Cody said.

"I wonder who he was," Taylor said. "He must have lived here."

"We gotta get rid of him," Peter said.

"But how? Any suggestions?" Cody flipped through the book. "How do people get rid of ghosts?"

"Exorcism," Nicole said. She took the book and checked the index.

"What's that?" Peter asked.

"It's sort of like a spell. 'You ring the bell, close the book, and quench the candle,'" she read from the book.

"'Quench'?" Peter said.

Nicole gave him a scornful look. "It means pinch out. Don't you know anything?"

"Yeah, but I thought 'quench' meant like quenching thirst."

"It means that, too."

"Maybe that's for witches," Taylor said. "Like that old movie *Bell, Book and Candle.*"

"Whatever," Nicole said. "It's for getting rid of the unwanted supernatural beings dwelling in a house."

"Don't we want to solve the mystery?" Taylor said.

For a while it looked like Peter and Cody were going to say no. Then Cody said he'd always wanted a real mystery to solve.

"You don't have to live in the middle of it," Peter pointed out, "but we do."

"If we get rid of the ghosts, we may never know why they are appearing or what the lady is searching for," Taylor said.

"Yeah, it might be gold," Cody said.

"Or treasure," Nicole said.

Peter looked torn between wanting to hunt treasure and being able to sleep in a ghost-free house. Finally, he said, "OK, let's vote on it. All those in favor of exorcism, raise your hands."

Peter raised his. Taylor watched to see what Nicole would do. Exorcism had been her idea. She would love dressing up in a long robe and telling ghosts to begone.

Nicole didn't raise her hand. Neither did Cody. Peter was the only one.

"OK, what's the next thing?" Cody turned a page and read, "'To give surcease to a tortured ghostly soul, try to find out why the ghost is appearing.' What does 'surcease' mean?"

Nicole ran to look it up. "It means to cease from an action, to come to an end," she reported.

"How do we do it?" Peter asked.

Cody was reading ahead. He didn't want to say.

"I know what it is," Nicole said. "A séance."

The way she said the word—hissing the s sounds, making her eyes look eerie—gave Taylor chills. Or maybe it was the coolness of the morning. But whichever it was, she felt spooked.

"That's right," Cody said. "One way to do that is a séance. The book says it right here." He pointed to the chapter heading: The Séance. He didn't look happy about it.

"We're going to have a séance," Nicole said before anybody could object.

"When?" Peter asked.

"Now," Nicole said.

"It's daytime," Peter objected. "Ghosts don't appear in the daytime."

"Well, actually they do." Cody looked up from the book. "They're not as easily seen because it's harder for them to—um, materialize in daylight. But it doesn't mean they're not there . . ." His voice dwindled.

"I saw that face in the attic window in daylight," Taylor said.

"Oh, man." Peter got up and walked the length of the porch and back. "I don't think so. I don't wanna do this."

"Let's vote on it," Taylor said. She didn't want to do it either. It was one thing to solve a ghost's problem—it was another to invite one to appear.

"No," Nicole said. "There's no point in voting. We have to do it. We'll get some information from it that will help us solve the problem. You don't want to live in a haunted house, do you, Peter?"

"No. I mean it's sort of neat, but I wouldn't want it to be a habit. What if these ghosts had friends and they started dropping by and first thing you know, we're running a ghost hotel."

"Very funny," Nicole said as Taylor and Cody grinned. "Read on, Cody. Are there instructions on how to have a séance?"

"'It should be held in the room where manifestations have been sighted.'"

"What are 'manifestations'?" Peter asked.

Taylor knew that one. "Ghosts."

He rolled his eyes at her. Peter seemed to think it was half a joke and half scary. Taylor felt that way, too, until she remembered seeing the ghosts. Then it was all-the-way scary.

"What else?" Nicole prodded.

"'A table, round if possible.'"

"We can do that."

"Where?" Cody asked. "We have to decide where."

"The ghosts have appeared in my room and the antique bedroom," Nicole said slowly, as if suddenly having second thoughts about the séance.

"I don't want to have it in the antique bedroom," Taylor said firmly. No way was she going to have a séance in there.

"No," Nicole agreed. "That wouldn't be a good place."

Actually it would be the perfect place with two ghosts hanging around, but Taylor wasn't going to be there if that was the room they picked. She would walk to New Mexico first.

"I don't think my room would be a good place either."

Taylor smiled. So did Cody and Peter. They were all thinking the same thing: Nicole didn't want ghosts hanging out in her room.

Nicole frowned and played with the end of her ponytail as they all tried to think of a suitable place.

"How about the upstairs hall? It's sort of neutral," Taylor said.

"I vote for the upstairs hall," Peter said.

"That's perfect," Nicole said. "OK, upstairs hall. We can use that round parlor table up there. We'll have to bring more chairs in. What else?"

Cody checked the séance rules. "Candles if it's dark."

"That's out." Nicole shook her head. "Mom would have a fit. We don't need them in the daylight."

"What time today?" Peter asked.

"Why not now?" Nicole said. Suddenly everybody but Nicole got busy. Taylor retied her sneaker. Peter scratched a bug bite. Cody flipped pages, then said he couldn't do a séance on an empty stomach.

"Me neither," Peter said.

"But it's just barely after breakfast," Nicole pointed out.

"True, but I'm already getting hungry," Peter said.

Nicole gave in. "How about two o'clock?"

Nobody could think of a reason that two wouldn't be the perfect time for the séance. "All right then. Everybody meet there at one-thirty to set it up." Nicole took the book from Cody to brush up on séance rules. Taylor was scared, but she didn't want to miss whatever was going to happen. Whatever it was, she wanted to be there to see it.

CHAPTER 12

THE GRAY CLOUDS HAD DARKENED TO SLATE BY LUNCHTIME. It was probably going to rain soon. Taylor wasn't hungry, but nothing seemed to bother Peter's appetite. Or Cody's. Taylor managed half a jelly sandwich while the boys wolfed down leftover spaghetti with clams. Clammy clams, Taylor thought as she stared out the window at trees bowing in the wind. That's probably how ectoplasm feels. Clammy like cold clams. Taylor had never touched a ghost, and she never planned to.

Sylvia came upstairs as they were finishing lunch and looked in the refrigerator. "It looks like a herd of hungry kids have been in here."

"Um, Mom, are you going to be cooking in here now?" Nicole asked as Sylvia started taking things out of the refrigerator.

"No, just sandwiches. Is it all right if Steve and I have a bite? Parents have to eat, too, you know."

"We'll make it for you and bring it downstairs on a tray," Nicole said.

"Nicole, do you have a fever?" Sylvia asked.

"No, this is Be Kind to Parents Hour." She looked at the kitchen clock. "And you only have fifteen minutes to take advantage of this amazing offer!"

"All right." Sylvia laughed. "Just remember, nothing too weird like onions and chocolate," she said as she went back downstairs to her office.

Nicole put everyone to work, and soon they had two BLTs with potato chips on plates and a pitcher of iced tea with two glasses ready to take downstairs. Everybody carried something as they delivered the lunch with a flourish.

"History is being made today," Dad said. He and Sylvia looked so touched that Taylor felt guilty. They should be kind to parents more often.

At one-thirty Taylor, Peter, and Cody each carried a chair from the kitchen to the upstairs hall. Nicole had disappeared soon after reminding them of the séance time, saying she had to prepare herself. "How do you prepare yourself for a séance?" Taylor asked the boys.

Peter shrugged. "You never know with Nicole. For a long while when she was little, she had to dress up like a nurse before she would go to the doctor. Then she started dressing like a doctor."

"What does she dress up like now?" Cody asked.

"Herself," Peter said. "We never know what that'll be."

It sounded to Taylor like Nicole just liked to get attention.

Somebody had dragged the round table into the center of the upstairs hall, placed a high-backed chair behind it, and draped it with a gold satin bedspread. Nicole's chair. They circled their chairs around the table and sat down to wait. Gloomy gray light seeped in from two windows at the front and back of the house.

Taylor was about to suggest getting cards for a game of hearts when Nicole appeared wearing a long purple robe that, on closer inspection, turned out to be another bedspread she had made into a cape and tied with a piece of gold drapery cord. Her long hair was down, and she wore something that looked like a cross between an Egyptian pharaoh's crown and parts of an old chandelier.

"Yard sales and dance costumes," Peter said under his breath as Taylor and Cody stared.

"Why are you dressed like that?" Taylor asked.

"To make the spirits feel comfortable," Nicole whispered.

"Why are you whispering?" Cody asked.

"To make the spirits feel comfortable," Peter whispered.

Everybody giggled except Nicole, who frowned at them. "You have to be serious," she reproved. "The spirits don't like to be laughed at. It makes them mad."

"Sorry, spirits," Peter said with a grin.

"Peter, if you can't be serious, we'll have to do this without you," Nicole said, forgetting to whisper.

"What are you going to do about it, tell Mom?"

She ignored that. "A séance is better with four. I've been reading about them. If you can't do it right, it's better not to do it at all."

"OK, OK. Let's get going."

"We have to wait until the clock strikes the hour."

"Is that in the book?" Taylor asked.

"No, but things always happen on the hour. Maybe that's the best time for spirits to come."

Her words hung in the air. "For spirits to come." Taylor suppressed a shiver. What was she doing in this darkening hall with Nicole dressed like something from an old movie trying to lure spirits out in the daytime and get them to reveal their secrets? Taylor didn't want any spirits to come. She wanted them to go away. Ghosts were scary.

"What do we do?" Peter asked.

"We have to hold hands and wait."

Nicole sat back in the chair with her hands on the table, her eyes closed. The boys choked back giggles as each took one of Taylor's hands and one of Nicole's. Now they were joined in a circle.

Downstairs in the hall, the grandfather clock struck twice.

Nicole cleared her throat. "Speak to us, spirits," she intoned in a spectral voice. "Tell us what is troubling you so we can help you."

Wind gusted around the outside of the house as the storm struck. Raindrops drilled the front windows and hammered the slate roof.

"Speak, spirits!" Nicole's voice rose against the storm.

Light leaked away, darkening the hall until it was almost as dark as dusk. Nicole flung her head back dramatically. The crown-chandelier tilted and threatened to slip down over her left eye. "Speak to us, spirits!"

Taylor wanted to giggle—Nicole looked so funny. Peter had his lips pressed together to keep from laughing. Cody stared at the table.

Just as Taylor was about to say, "Guess nobody is coming," a figure rose behind the table, a figure that appeared out of the air.

Taylor shivered and gasped. It was the lady they had seen in Nicole's room and in the antique bedroom. Here, even in the dusky light, she could see the lady's face for the first time: the dark brown hair drawn from a center part into two braids that wound around over each ear, the black corseted bodice of her long-sleeved dress, the skirt with a bustle in the back. Taylor's eyes were drawn to her face. Her skin was pale and lined, her eyes dark and anguished. She wrung a white handkerchief with a black border in her hand.

Nicole's eyes were open as she whispered again, "Speak to us," in a strangled voice.

The lady opened her eyes, then seemed to look beyond them. Her mouth opened. Something crashed to the ground outside and she was gone. For a minute, still holding hands, nobody spoke. Then everybody talked at once.

"Did you see that?"

"She was going to speak!"

"She heard you!"

"Her mouth was open to speak!"

"She saw something. Something that scared her away."

"No, she heard the crash!"

Peter jumped up and turned on the hall light. "It's too weird in here."

Nobody disagreed.

The séance had been a success and a failure.

"The ghost appeared but we didn't learn anything," Cody said.

"Not necessarily," Nicole said. "We learned that we can summon a ghost."

"Maybe she was going to appear anyway," Taylor said. "Maybe she appears all the time and we just don't see her because it's too light or we're making too much noise or something."

"Don't be silly. Of course she came because I called her," Nicole said. "Let's try again."

Nobody wanted to.

"If we don't, we're never going to find out anything," Nicole argued.

"OK." Peter turned off the light. They joined hands again, and Nicole called out to the spirits.

Taylor's hands felt like ice. It was hard to hold Peter's hand in the cast. He kept squeezing her fingers. Cody's hand was limp on the other side. Taylor's poison ivy began to itch. She scratched her right leg with her other foot.

"Be still," Nicole hissed.

"My ear itches," Peter said. "I think I caught Taylor's poison ivy."

"You can't catch it," Cody said.

"Quiet!" Nicole ordered.

"You're not the boss of me," Peter began, when suddenly a figure loomed in front of the bathroom door. This one wore white—a long white nightgown—and her plaits were down and she looked younger. But she was the same person. The same ghost.

They watched her in silence as her lips opened and formed the beginning of a word: "Ja—"

The room temperature suddenly dropped what seemed like fifty degrees. Pixels of light swirled into the figure of a man. He seemed to glow like an ice sculpture. Then just as suddenly he disappeared. The woman whooshed abruptly down the stairs, as if she'd been blown by a huge wind.

All four of them jumped up and ran downstairs, where the ghost had stopped at the front door. She fell to her knees on a rag rug and disappeared.

They stared at the spot where the woman had knelt on the rag rug. The floor in front of the door was bare.

CHAPTER

13

"WHAT'S GOING ON HERE?" CODY BENT DOWN AND TOUCHED the bare floor. "Where did the rug go?"

"It didn't go anywhere," Nicole said.

"There wasn't any rug," Peter said. "The floor has been bare since we moved in. Mom said she wanted to get one but she hasn't seen anything she liked."

"Maybe it's a ghost rug," Cody said.

"Something must have happened on that rug," Taylor said.

"She looked like she was mourning someone," Nicole said.

The séance had been a bust for information. They hadn't learned anything except that the house was definitely haunted by two ghosts and that the woman appeared at two different times in her life and something must have happened at the front door. That didn't explain why ghosts were walking around upstairs. It didn't tell them who the woman ghost was. Or the man. Or why the woman appeared young in the nightgown and older in the black dress.

"I think he was a Civil War soldier," Taylor said. "He looked like the ones I've seen pictures of at battlefields like Manassas and Gettysburg."

"Was he a Confederate soldier?" Taylor asked Cody. "I couldn't tell."

"I couldn't either," Cody said. "Sometimes the uniforms were hard to tell apart. You have to look for the insignia, US or CSA. But in the early part of the war, they didn't even wear insignias and their uniforms were often the same color."

"Wow, that must have been confusing on the battlefields," Peter said.

"Yeah, and even when they wore different uniforms it was confusing. General Stonewall Jackson was shot by his own men at Chancellorsville. They thought he was Union," Cody said.

"They must have felt bad killing their own general," Peter said.

"Yeah. It was bad for the Confederacy. He was one of the best generals. Anyway, Stonewall didn't die right away. They had to cut his arm off. They buried it there in a graveyard. My cousin's seen it. It has a tombstone just like a regular grave. When Stonewall died a few days later, they buried the rest of him somewhere else."

"Maybe the soldier we saw was shot, and the lady tried to help him," Nicole suggested.

"He didn't look like he needed any help," Peter said.

"He looked like the kind of soldier you'd run from," Taylor said. "The kind that would shoot you."

"Let's try again," Nicole said. "We need more info."

But the storm had passed, and Cody's mother called for him to come home. Nicole flounced off in her robe and crown, snatching the bedspread from her chair on the way to her room. Taylor and Peter were left to drag all the chairs back to the kitchen, where they ran into Sylvia.

"Oh, just in time to clean up the yard for me," she said. "We have millions of things to do before July Daze. We didn't need this storm to leave the yard in such a mess." She gestured at the fallen limbs and branches and other debris left by the storm on the lawn and in the flower beds. "How is your writing coming along, Taylor?"

"Writing?" For a moment Taylor didn't know what she meant. It must be something about the festival. Then she remembered Dad had volunteered her to write about the house. "Oh, er, fine. It's coming along."

They got rakes from the barn and a yard cart and filled it with leaves blown from gutters, broken limbs, and millions of sticks. Everything smelled fresh and clean and wet after the storm. It was fun to be outside moving around, even if it was work. But why didn't Nicole have to help?

"She's a genius at disappearing when there are jobs to do," Peter said.

When the last of the sticks, leaves, and twigs had been raked and picked up, Taylor sat down on the porch with the book she had brought back from the library and looked at it. *The History of Warfield County.* She flipped through the pages. They were old and yellowed, and the print was small. She looked at the illustrations—black-and-white photographs of the Warfield County courthouse, a wagon loaded with cotton, a log cabin, then houses with names like Greengage, Montmorada, Rowan Forest, Stone's Throw. Some of the houses were wooden, some stone, some brick. Maybe this house was in the book. Taylor turned to the index, and there it was, Swain's Fancy. She found the page and an old black-and-white photo of the house, dated 1927. Taylor began to read.

She kept what she had found in the book to herself until after supper when Cody came over. "We have to have a meeting," she said. "Let's sit on the front steps. That's close to where it happened."

"Where what happened?" Peter asked as they all sat below Taylor and waited for her to begin. A single firefly glittered in the gathering dusk near the summerhouse.

Nicole was quiet. She probably didn't like Taylor having everybody's attention. Taylor showed them the book. "I started reading it for the history I have to write, and I found out who the ghost is." She paused.

"Go on," Cody urged.

"Her name was Elizabeth Maria Swain, and she was born in this house in 1843. Her father was Thomas Swain, great-grandson of Abel Swain, who built this house in 1754. Her mother died when she was little, and her father never married again, but he took in two orphaned boys who were distant relatives and raised them as his own. Jason and Jared Swain were brothers only a year apart. They looked a lot alike, and both were in love with Elizabeth. Elizabeth had grown up with both and didn't know which one to choose. When the Civil War started, what's now West Virginia was still Virginia. In this part of the state, the Eastern Panhandle of West Virginia, people were divided about three to one between the Confederacy and the Union. The farms in the Shenandoah Valley supplied food for the Confederate troops. President Lincoln was determined to keep the upper part of the Valley in the Union. There was a lot of fighting back and forth. Some families were divided, with part of them Union and part Confederate. Thomas Swain was neither, because he was a Quaker. He belonged to the Society of Friends. That was a religious denomination that was Pacifist, which means they didn't believe in killing or war," Taylor explained. She'd had to look it up. "There were a lot of bad feelings in the Eastern Panhandle. The brothers had become rivals for Elizabeth by the time the war started. Jared joined the Confederacy, and Jason joined the Union army."

"Lots of families were divided around here," Cody said. "My great-great-great-grandfathers fought on opposite sides."

"The soldier we saw was one of the brothers?" Peter asked. "Jared or Jason?"

Taylor nodded.

"What happened to them?"

Nicole hadn't said a word through all of this. Her attention was on the firefly by the summerhouse.

"The Battle of Winchester happened," Taylor said. "One of them."

"How many were there?" Peter asked.

"A lot. The first one, I think, was in 1862." She flipped through the pages. "Yes, here it is: May 25, 1862. General Stonewall Jackson and General Richard Ewell attacked the Union army under General Nathaniel Banks and the Union army retreated to Harper's Ferry. That's in West Virginia, which had just seceded from Virginia."

"You mean part of a state seceded from a state that had seceded from the Union?" Peter asked.

"That's what happened," Taylor said. "It's pretty confusing. But the whole Civil War was. Anyway, Jason and Jared were both there, fighting on opposite sides. The Confederates won and the Union army retreated. Jason was wounded, but he was able to ride his horse back to safety at Swain's Fancy. Elizabeth nursed Jason and while he was recuperating, she realized he was the one she loved. After a while, Jared found out he was here and came to capture him, but Thomas said no, this was his house and their home and it was neutral ground. They could stay in the house as before. That night, Jason and an accomplice stole Thomas's gold from where he had it hidden in the attic step that's taller than the others. The fifth step. He was escaping with it when Jared caught him and shot him there at the front door. He didn't know it was his brother. He was shooting at a thief."

Nobody spoke, but Taylor knew they were all thinking the same thing, that Elizabeth was the ghost who had knelt on the rug at the front door. The ghost of Jason had gone down first. He'd dissolved before they got down the stairs, so only Elizabeth was left kneeling at the door.

"She must have run downstairs in her nightgown when she heard the shot," Taylor continued. "It was too late. Jason was dead. The bag of gold was under him when he fell. They only found half of the gold. Jared shot at his accomplice but missed, and the man got away with the other bag of gold."

"Wow! All this happened right here at our front door," Peter said in amazement.

"So what happened?" Cody asked. "Did Elizabeth marry Jared?"

"No. She never married anybody. Jared tried to get her to marry him but she refused. She said Jason was innocent and searched for the rest of her life for something that would prove it. Jared finally gave up in"—she checked the book— "1872 and married somebody else. But all his children died as babies, and then his wife died. He tried again to get Elizabeth to marry him but she never did. They both died in 1910, and the house was sold."

"So now we know who the ghosts are," Peter said. "Elizabeth and Jason. It was Jason we saw in the hall at the séance. He probably had the gold on him then."

"Now maybe we can solve Elizabeth's problem so she will stop haunting the house," Cody said. "And then maybe Jason will go away, too. Good work, Taylor."

"Yeah, cool," Peter said.

Nicole said nothing. Taylor was disappointed in her lack of interest. She had been so excited to find out who their ghosts were, to solve the mystery.

Nicole acted as if she hadn't even heard the story. She stared at the summerhouse. Then she spoke. "There's somebody out there," she said in a whisper, pointing.

"Where?" The boys followed her. Taylor peered through the dusk at the shadowy summerhouse. "I don't see anything," she said.

Nicole jumped up and ran to the pond, with the boys behind her. Taylor was left alone on the steps with the book. She didn't believe anybody was in the summerhouse. Nicole was jealous because she had solved the mystery, jealous because Taylor had found out something she didn't know. Nicole had to turn the attention to herself.

Well, they would find out it was just another of her tricks. Taylor waited. The shadows deepened and swallowed the summerhouse. She watched as fireflies glittered as thick as stars. But the boys didn't come back, and neither did Nicole, and Taylor knew that the trick had been played on her. All her excitement at finding out the identity of the ghosts dissolved and she was left feeling disappointed in Nicole. She had thought they'd become sort of friends. She resolved never to be fooled by Nicole again.

CHAPTER

14

NICOLE DIDN'T COME TO THE ANTIQUE BEDROOM THAT NIGHT. Taylor waited out in the hall. She wasn't going to sleep in that double-haunted room alone. Not with Jason roaming around. She knocked on Nicole's door.

"What do you want?" Nicole said through the door.

"Are you going to sleep in the other room?" Taylor asked, already knowing the answer.

"No. Now that I know who the ghost in my room is, I'll sleep here by myself. Elizabeth is a friendly ghost."

"Can I sleep there, too?"

"No. You have a room of your own."

Taylor tried the knob. The door was locked. Suddenly she was furious. Was she making Taylor sleep alone in the antique room with Jason's scary ghost because she was jealous? That was no reason.

Nicole got her way about everything, but this time she would show Nicole. She wouldn't let her get away with this.

She'd get that note and show it to Dad and Sylvia. Nicole would be in big trouble.

Taylor stomped into the antique bedroom. She turned on the lamp. Where had she put that note? She went over the events of that night in her mind. Nicole had scribbled the note, then given it to her. She had tossed it on the nightstand. They had read awhile, then turned out the light, and the ghost of Elizabeth had appeared. That was the last time she remembered seeing the note. Now the top of the nightstand was bare except for a pile of books. Taylor sat on the bed and flipped through each book to see if she'd slipped the note into one of them.

Nothing.

She held each book up and fanned the pages to make the note fall out. Again nothing. Taylor checked the trunk and the chest of drawers. The trunk was half full of bedding that smelled of lavender. The drawers were empty. No note anywhere.

Nicole had probably sneaked back in and taken the note. Taylor wanted to tell her dad what was going on, but now she couldn't prove there had been a note. Nicole would deny everything. Taylor would be the one to look mean instead of Nicole. And the grown-ups would find out about the ghost hunt. Taylor had never been as mad at anybody as she was at Nicole now, but she couldn't think of anything to do about it.

She got into bed and read until she was sleepy. That took

a long time because she was still seething. Finally her eyelids felt so heavy she couldn't keep them open. She barely remembered to turn off the lamp as the book slipped down on the covers.

The strange greenish light that surrounded Elizabeth's ghost woke her. Taylor's eyes flew open as Elizabeth moved around the room, searching in phantom furniture.

"What are you looking for, Elizabeth?" Taylor asked.

The ghost didn't seem to hear her. She went on with her search. Taylor sat up to watch. Elizabeth didn't seem to see her. She was intent on her quest. It was as if Taylor were the ghost.

"Why do you come here every night? Did you search before I came or does your search have something to do with me?"

No reply. Taylor hadn't really expected one, and she was glad this ghost didn't speak to her. Elizabeth moved toward the bed, then stopped and finally disappeared through the door. Taylor stared into the darkness. There had to be a connection. The other houses in *The History of Warfield County* had stories of ghosts. But no ghosts had been mentioned about Swain's Fancy. That was odd, since there were two, Elizabeth and Jason.

Jason! It was time for his appearance. Taylor didn't think she could bear to see him in the room by herself. She swung her feet over the side of the bed.

Too late!

The temperature in the room dropped as light appeared in the center of the room. The house was silent as bluish pixels swirled like a swarm of fireflies. They formed themselves into a man, a man in a Civil War uniform. In the dark room she couldn't tell what uniform he wore but it had to be Jason, the thief!

Taylor tried to scream. She opened her mouth, but no sound came out. Her throat was paralyzed, frozen. She was cold. Chills ran up and down her spine as the soldier advanced toward her, staring at her. His eyes were the bluest and coldest she had ever seen, cobalt eyes that seemed to burn through her like an icy laser.

The ghost moved purposefully toward the bed, his terrible eyes locked onto hers. Taylor couldn't look away. Her eyes were trapped. She couldn't move. She was paralyzed all over now with cold, with terror.

He came closer, closer. He raised his right arm. Something glinted in his hand. He seemed to be pointing it. Taylor focused on his hand. He was pointing a gun!

Taylor had to get away. Her breath came in tiny shallow gasps. It felt like she was breathing ice splinters into her lungs. She didn't know how much longer she would be able to breathe this cold before she suffocated. She had to get away.

With a sob, Taylor reached deep into her lungs for a breath and rolled off the bed. She hit the floor and kept rolling to the door, away from the terrible face of the ghost.

He saw her fall and turned to change his direction. He took a step toward her.

The doorknob seemed a million miles away. Taylor reached up, up, up. Her fingers hit the knob. She pulled herself upright and wrenched the knob. Please turn, she whispered soundlessly. It seemed to be stuck. Taylor turned with her weight on the knob. She could feel the cold of the ghost coming closer. She didn't dare take the time or waste her energy checking to see how near he had come or what he was doing behind her.

Why wouldn't the knob move? Was it frozen, too? Taylor yanked it the other way and pushed against the door, as much to get away from the cold as to open the door. A sheet of ice seemed to be pushing against her as the ghost came closer.

The door was like a stone wall.

CHAPTER
15

DESPERATELY, TAYLOR TWISTED THE KNOB ONE MORE TIME. The ghost was almost on her. The air pulsated behind her in frigid waves, as if the ghost were breathing icy air onto her. That was impossible. He was a ghost. He couldn't breathe. Could he? "Help me!" Taylor gasped. Her voice was no more than a whisper.

The knob turned. Taylor threw herself against the door as hard as she could. It opened, and she was in the hall. But not safe. Not yet. She had only gained a few seconds. She remembered the séance. The ghost had probably come out of that room. He wasn't confined to it. He could follow her into the hall.

Taylor shut the door behind her, forgetting that a closed door wouldn't stop the ghost. She ran across the hall to Peter's room, stumbling against his door. She jerked it open without knocking and burst into the room.

"Peter!" she whispered loudly.

Maybe she would be safe in Peter's room. Nobody had seen any manifestations there. Not yet.

"Huh? What—?"

Taylor felt around for a light switch, knocking something over and tripping over something else.

"Who's that?"

Peter switched on the lamp. "Taylor! What's happening? You look like you've seen a ghost."

"Jason. Jason is in my room. And he's horrible, Peter, just horrible. I couldn't get out of there. He was going to kill me."

"Where is he now?" Peter looked past her to see if Jason was coming through the door. Taylor turned around to check. The door was closed, but it wouldn't stop that horrible ghost.

"I don't know. I left him in my room. I think he was still there. He came into the hall at the séance—he could be out there by now. I don't think he comes in here, so can I stay for the night?"

"I guesso. Sure." Peter looked worried.

"I won't snore or anything." Taylor didn't plan to sleep. She would probably never sleep a wink in this house again.

"It's not that. Is there something we can do to make sure the ghost doesn't come in here?"

Taylor shook her head. She was suddenly tired, as if she had been walking for miles in subzero temperatures. The cold had drained her energy. She got in the other twin bed, propped herself up on the pillow, and watched the door.

Peter did the same, and asked her what the ghost had done.

"I don't want to talk about him tonight." Taylor was too tired to talk. She was too tired to think. And she certainly didn't want to think about that horrible ghost.

In a few minutes Peter made a purring sound. How could he sleep with a ghost in the hall?

SYLVIA POSTED A LIST ON THE REFRIGERATOR DOOR. "OK, everybody, we're on a deadline for the festival. Here's the list of things to do. Peter and Nicole will start weeding this morning while it's cool. I want to have a reasonable facsimile of a garden when people come on the tour. Steve is bringing blooming plants from the nursery, and we'll distribute those around the garden to give it lots of color."

"What about Taylor?" Nicole asked. "Isn't she going to weed, too?"

"Taylor, I want you to finish up the story of the house you're working on. Can you have it done by tomorrow?"

Taylor nodded. "I think so."

"Good. Because there's plenty of other work to be done." Sylvia rushed off to her office.

Taylor poured cereal and milk in a bowl and added banana slices. Peter made toast. Taylor sat across from Nicole and picked up her spoon.

Peter scraped jam on his toast. Taylor crunched her cereal. It sounded loud. Peter crunched his toast. It sounded even louder. He looked miffed. Nicole looked mad.

Taylor was mad, too, but for different reasons.

"You think you're getting away with something, getting to goof off with your writing." Nicole minced the last three words and made a face.

"At least I'm not a thief," Taylor replied with all the anger stored up from last night.

"What do you mean 'thief'?"

"You know what I mean."

"I'm not a thief. Liar."

Taylor wouldn't say any more. She got up and rinsed her bowl. She put it in the dishwasher while Nicole glowered. Peter crunched toast. Seething, Taylor went down to e-mail her mother.

She didn't want to tell her mom about the ghosts, but she had to tell somebody about Nicole. So she just said that something Nicole had given her was missing from her room and she thought Nicole had taken it back.

She clicked on "Send" and waited for her mother's reply. She only had to wait minutes. Mom said that whatever it was could have fallen behind something or blown somewhere or she could have picked it up with a pile of something. *That happens a lot,* she wrote. *Please don't get into a fight. You and Nicole should be friends. Remember, you're stepsisters now for life.*

It sounded like a sentence.

OK, I'll look some more, Taylor typed.

I won't be mad until I know for sure.

But Nicole was mad at her. She thought Taylor was getting out of all the hard work. If Taylor did what Sylvia asked, Nicole would really hate her. She could go out and pull weeds to show Nicole she wasn't trying to get out of anything. Then Nicole would be controlling what she did. Either way, she couldn't win.

Taylor opened the history book and read about the house again. She tried to think of a way to write the story of Swain's Fancy that would be more interesting to read than this dry account. She decided to write it as a love story.

It was 1862. Elizabeth Swain had to choose between her father's two wards, the brothers Jared and Jason Swain.

Taylor typed for almost an hour, ending the story with Elizabeth's living in the house for the rest of her life without ever marrying. Taylor had a lot of questions.

Why didn't Elizabeth marry Jared? Did he look too much like Jason? Why did she spend the rest of her life looking for proof of Jason's innocence? The bag of stolen gold was found under him. His accomplice got away with the other bag. Why would Elizabeth think he was innocent? It was a mystery, a soap opera. Suddenly Taylor had an idea.

She clicked on "Print" and made four copies of her

account. She gave one to Sylvia in her office. "It's not finished yet," she said. "I want to add some more to the end."

Sylvia glanced at the pages. "Looks good. Thanks."

Taylor went outside. Nicole and Peter were weeding along the side of the house in a long border bed of pink, red, and white hollyhocks, dropping the weeds into a bushel basket. They looked hot. Peter's face was red from the heat. Nicole's turned red when she saw Taylor.

"Listen, I've just had a great idea," Taylor began.

Nicole jumped up, holding the basket. "We don't want to hear your ideas."

"Why not? It's a really good one."

"You think you're so smart. Well, you're not. I wish my mom had never married your dad. I wish you'd go back to Washington where you belong. We don't want you here."

"I never did anything to you," Taylor said.

"You're here. That's enough," Nicole said.

"At least I never stole anything from you."

"I never stole anything from you either," Nicole retorted.

"Yes you did. You stole back that note you signed."

"I did not!"

"Yes you did!"

"Liar!" Nicole raised the basket, and before Taylor realized what she was about to do, before she could duck, Nicole flung the contents at her. Weeds and dirt rained over Taylor's head.

Peter stared. "What did you do that for?"

"Now you can pick up the weeds," Nicole said to Taylor, and stomped off to the house.

Taylor's face was full of dirt. She shook herself like a dog after a bath but instead of water, dirt and weeds flew off her. Peter plucked more weeds out of her hair and off her shoulders. Taylor swiped at her face, spitting out her anger with the dirt.

"She's real mad at you," Peter said.

"No kidding!"

"What did she steal?"

"Just something. She made a promise and then she broke it. She stole the paper the promise was written on."

"She usually keeps her word," Peter said.

"Well, she didn't this time."

Taylor brushed the top page of the printout. She peeled off two pages and gave them to Peter to read. "This is what I wrote. I had a really great idea but now I don't want to do anything with Nicole ever again. I hate her. I divorce her from being my stepsister."

"I don't like her sometimes either, but I don't think she would steal back a promise."

"Well, if she didn't take the note, who did? Because it's not there."

Peter didn't have an answer.

The dirt and weeds made her feel itchy again. Taylor had to take a shower, and it wasn't even bedtime. She would finish the story for Sylvia and forget her ideas. She would forget about the ghosts. She would go back to Washington as soon as she could, and Nicole could live in the house with the ghost of Jason to terrify her. With Taylor gone, maybe he would start haunting Nicole's room. That would fix her.

Taylor put on clean shorts and a roomy green T-shirt. When she came downstairs, Nicole was picking up the rest of the weeds. Peter was in the kitchen pouring himself a tall glass of lemonade from a pitcher with mint sprigs bobbing around the ice. Nicole came in, still red. Taylor was mad, too. She turned her back to Nicole and poured a glass for herself.

"I didn't steal the note." Nicole sat down at the table and picked up the pages Taylor had given Peter. She fanned herself with them.

"If you didn't, then who did? It's gone, disappeared. I've looked everywhere."

"I don't know." Nicole stopped fanning. "The last time I saw it, it was on the table by the bed."

"Well, it's not there now."

They glared at each other.

"Maybe the ghost took it," Peter offered.

Taylor turned around and looked at him. So did Nicole. Then they looked at each other.

"Maybe he did," Nicole said.

"Or caused it to disappear somewhere," Taylor said.

"Let's go look," Peter said.

They ran upstairs to the antique bedroom. Peter looked through the books in the room.

"I already did that," Taylor told him.

"Sometimes things get stuck."

She noticed that he had started reading the Jeeves and Wooster book.

"Peter, stop reading right now," Nicole ordered. "You can read those books later."

Taylor and Nicole searched the drawers, the trunk under the bed, the bedclothes. They even moved the furniture, but no note appeared. Finally, when there was nowhere else to look, they stopped.

"I guess we'd better put all the furniture and stuff back," Nicole said. But as they slid the nightstand beside the bed, a pen fell behind it. Taylor bent to pick it up and saw the corner of a piece of paper stuck between the wall and the baseboard.

CHAPTER 16

"WHAT IS THIS?" TAYLOR REACHED FOR THE CORNER OF THE paper, but it slid farther behind the baseboard.

"We need tweezers," Nicole said.

"I'll get them." Peter ran to the bathroom and returned with a pair. Taylor tweezed the corner of the paper. It was the promise Nicole had signed.

"I'm sorry I thought you took it," Taylor said.

"I can see why you would think that," Nicole said. "It was really hidden behind there. Who would ever think to look behind a baseboard?"

Taylor looked at the note. She didn't want it now. She had almost forgotten why she ever had. The craterous face of Abel Swain seemed to belong to another time. Now they had real ghosts to worry about.

"Here," she said, handing the note to Nicole. "You can have it back. I don't need it now."

"No, you keep it. A promise is a promise."

"Then I don't need the note," Taylor said, and she tore the paper into tiny bits. As she was about to drop them in her pocket, the room cooled suddenly.

"Run!" Taylor yelled, but it was too late. The ghost of Jason Swain loomed in front of the door, blocking their escape. They were trapped!

They huddled behind the bed as the ghost seemed to grow even bigger. He wore a Civil War uniform and carried a pistol. His blue eyes blazed with hate and rage as he advanced toward them, lifting the pistol as he prepared to take aim.

Peter clutched Taylor. Taylor held on to Nicole.

"He's going to k-k-kill us," Peter said.

"We've got to g-get out of here," Nicole said.

"B-but how?"

The ghost looked at them as they cowered. Then he began to fade and was gone almost as suddenly as he had appeared.

"Let's go," Peter said, heading for the door.

"No," Taylor said.

"Wha-at?" Peter and Nicole yelped.

"No, that's what he wants us to do. That's why he went away. He heard us say we wanted to get out of here."

Then Taylor realized what she had said. The ghost of Jason could hear them and understand what they were saying. Chills ran up and down her spine and spread all over her. Her scalp prickled.

"That's so scary," Nicole said in a whisper. Peter looked sick as he had the same realization.

"Let's think about that later," Taylor said. "There's something in this room he doesn't want us to find. He knew we wanted to get out so he went away to let us."

"So let's go," Peter said.

"No, that's what he wants us to do. Are we going to let a ghost tell us what to do?" Taylor asked.

"Yes!" Peter and Nicole said together.

"Think about this. Remember what the ghost book said. It takes a lot of energy to materialize. Especially for a ghost that angry. The cold he brings takes even more energy. He probably can't come back for a while. So let's search the room again while he's waiting for the juice to come back."

Peter didn't want to but Nicole thought it was a good idea. "Maybe if we find what he's trying to keep from us, he'll go away."

"What could it be?" Peter said. "We've searched this whole room. Taylor searched it before. There's nothing here."

"Maybe there is," Nicole said. "If the note fell behind the baseboard, maybe something else did, too."

"Hey, is anybody home?" Cody called from the front door.

Peter went down to let him in and bring him up to date on what was happening. They rushed back upstairs to join in the hunt. Peter was enthusiastic now that they had reinforcements.

They divided the room up and each took a wall to search behind the baseboard.

"What do you think it is?" Cody said as he ran a fingernail behind the edge of the board.

"I bet it's a treasure map," Peter said. "We could buy a canoe for the pond."

"We need more light," Nicole complained, and Peter got his flashlight and one from downstairs. They took turns using the lights.

They found nothing.

"What about the attic step?" Cody said. "Where the gold was hidden."

They checked the attic stairs. Taylor tugged at the top of the fifth stair from the bottom—the one that was steeper. "It's hinged," she said.

They crowded closer. "I bet there's gold in it," Peter said.

Cody shined the flashlight into the yawning rectangle. Empty. Disappointed, they returned to the antique room.

Taylor began to feel uneasy. How long did it take a ghost to recharge his ectoplasmic energy?

"Let's go around again," Cody said.

They switched sides. This time Taylor and Nicole took the baseboard behind the bed. "I think it's back here somewhere," Taylor said. "Every time Jason appears in this room, somebody is close to this wall, either in bed or when we were looking for the note. I think we should all concentrate on it."

"Maybe we could take the baseboard off," Peter said.

"Mom would have a fit," Nicole said. "She doesn't even want the plaster repaired in here. It has to be 'pristinely original,' she said. She's going to take the lamp out and put antique covers on the bed for the festival."

"We need something flat to probe with," Cody said.

"I have something," Peter said. He went to his room and brought back two flexible metal rulers.

"Let's look behind the bed and the stand," Nicole said.

She took one of the rulers and pushed it behind the baseboard where the note had been. Cody probed behind the bed.

"Let me try," Taylor said.

Nicole gave her the ruler. She pushed it down against the wall, back and forth.

Again and again she probed and pushed. The ruler skidded against something, then moved on. Taylor tried again.

Nicole, watching intently, said, "Did you find something?"

The boys crowded around.

Taylor pulled the ruler out and tried again, bending it to pull whatever was behind the board up so that Nicole could get it with the tweezers. It felt like a sheet of paper.

The ruler came up without any paper. Taylor tried again. This time the tip of the corner of a piece of paper rose between the wall and baseboard before slipping down again.

"It's there!" Taylor said. "It's really there. Get ready with the tweezers, Nicole."

She pushed the ruler down again and brought up the corner tip. Nicole was waiting. She pinched the tip with the tweezers and slowly moved them upward.

"Careful, it might be old. It could tear easily," Taylor said.

"I know that," Nicole said. She brought the paper up far enough to pull it the rest of the way with her fingers.

"What is it?" Peter and Cody leaned toward the wall.

The air suddenly cooled.

"Let's get out of here!" Peter shouted.

Nicole clutched the paper, and they ran into the hall.

"Where can we go?" Cody said.

"My room," Peter said. "He never comes in there."

"He might know that we've found what he was guarding," Taylor pointed out. Where could they go to be safe from the malevolent ghost?

CHAPTER 17

"THE SUMMERHOUSE," TAYLOR SAID.

"What?" Cody said.

Taylor didn't know why she had said it. The word had just popped into her head. "We can go to the summerhouse and be safe from Jason's ghost."

"Let's go then." Peter went first as they clattered downstairs and out the front door. Nicole ran with the note and was the first one across the bridge. She sat on the circular bench facing the house and waited for the others. "Hurry up, I want to know what this says."

They caught up with her and sat down.

Nicole handed the note to Taylor. "Here, you read it. You were the one who found it."

Taylor unfolded the note. Her fingertips tingled. She felt a presence with them in the summerhouse, but it wasn't the evil Jason's.

Jason,

Meet me in the summerhouse at midnight.

E

"That's all?" Peter's dreams of treasure dissolved.

Cody looked disappointed.

Nicole had no expression.

Taylor didn't know what to think. "Why would Jason go to such trouble to keep us from finding this note?"

Nicole shrugged.

They all had a let-down feeling. They had thought the note would solve the mystery and they could stop the ghosts from haunting Swain's Fancy. Now they were just as mystified as they had been before.

"Let's go through what we know," Taylor said. "Every detail about the story. We must be missing something."

"It's pretty simple. Jason and Jared both loved Elizabeth," Nicole said. "Jason joined the Union army and Jared the Confederate in the Civil War. Jason was wounded in the first Battle of Winchester in 1862. The Confederates won so he had to get away to keep from being captured. He came back here to get well, and Elizabeth fell in love with him." She stopped.

"The antique bedroom," Taylor said. "That must have been his room. That's why he haunts it."

"He needed money to run away with Elizabeth so he stole the bags of gold," Nicole said.

"No, he only stole one bag," Peter said. "He had an accomplice who got away with the other bag. Maybe they had it planned that way all along. Maybe he wasn't even really wounded."

"That would have come out after he was killed," Cody pointed out. "They would have known if he hadn't had a wound."

"That's true," Peter said.

"But that doesn't make sense," Taylor said. "Elizabeth loved him. She didn't have any sisters or brothers. She would inherit all the gold, and Swain's Fancy, too. Why didn't he just marry her and wait for it?"

"Maybe she wouldn't marry him," Cody suggested.

"'She loved him and believed he wasn't guilty despite the evidence of the bag of gold found under him,'" Taylor said, quoting the book. "Maybe he wasn't guilty. Maybe that's behind the whole thing."

"What whole thing?" Peter asked.

"The hauntings. Elizabeth searches the room Jason was in—the attic—and Nicole's room. That must have been Jared's room. She never searches Peter's room, because that was probably where her father slept. Nobody would have gone in there. The bathroom is in the other room. That must have been Elizabeth's. Nobody searches it. There's no need to."

"Or if they do, we haven't seen them," Nicole said.

They were all quiet for a moment, hoping there were no ghosts in the bathroom.

"I'm never going in there again," Peter said.

"Oh, you will," Nicole said. "If we haven't seen any ghosts in there, it's probably because they don't have a reason to be there. So you're safe."

"Don't forget what we saw at the séance," Cody said. "The old Elizabeth came out of Nicole's room. Where did the young Elizabeth come from? Where did Jason come from? And what about Jared?"

"We've forgotten about him. The soldier at the séance must have been Jared, because he had a gun and was going down to shoot Jason," Nicole said.

"But that can't be right," Peter said. "Jason had a gun in the antique bedroom today. And if he had a gun, why did he let Jared shoot him first?"

"He didn't have a gun," Taylor said. "The account said that he wasn't armed."

"So here's what must have happened," Cody said. "Elizabeth sent Jason a note to meet her in the summerhouse. He stole the gold and was going to get her to run away with him. He gave the gun to his accomplice, along with the second bag of gold."

"Yeah, I bet that's how it happened," Peter said.

"It could have happened that way," Nicole said. "That would explain why Elizabeth never told about the note."

"Maybe so," Taylor said.

They watched dragonflies and butterflies hovering over the green pond water, still as glass.

"What was your idea?" Peter said.

"What idea?" Taylor looked at him blankly.

"When we were weeding earlier and you came out and said you had a great idea. Just before Nicole—you know."

"Oh, that idea. I just thought that we could put on a little playlet about what happened at Swain's Fancy. You and Cody could play the brothers, and Nicole could be Elizabeth, and I could be the narrator or something."

"A play! That's a great idea." Nicole jumped up and started over the bridge. "I bet there are costumes in the attic. Let's go look."

"Wait, I have to write it first," Taylor said.

"Come on, you can write it as we go along," Nicole said.

The boys followed. As Taylor got up, something pushed at her. The wind? But there was no breeze—the pond surface was flat and reflective.

Dad was working in the barn, so Taylor went downstairs to use his computer. First she e-mailed Mom that she had found the lost note and she and Nicole were friends, and told her about the play. Then she pulled up the account she had already written and turned it into dialogue. She could work on it more as they rehearsed. She made copies of the play and the note Elizabeth had written to Jason on Dad's copy machine.

Nicole and the boys had brought down loads of old clothes from the attic and some from Nicole's stash in her room. They spread everything out in the family room. Sylvia was dismayed when she saw the disorder.

Nicole explained their plan.

Sylvia was instantly enthusiastic. "That's a wonderful idea. I'll have it added to the program. What is the play called?"

"The Mystery at Swain's Fancy," Taylor replied, without hesitation.

Nicole and Cody and Peter looked at Taylor inquiringly.

"We'll have to do it as a mystery, since we don't know the answer," she explained.

"Have you finished your account for the program, Taylor?" Sylvia asked.

"I can't finish it because I don't know the ending."

"I have to have it printed now. It seems complete to me."

Sylvia didn't know about the ghosts. Taylor shrugged. "OK. It's as much as anybody knows."

Taylor gave everybody a copy of the play. She would work more on the lines, but for now Nicole was in charge.

"Who wants to be Jason?" she asked the boys.

"Not me," Peter said.

"I will. I like being the villain," Cody said. He tried to look fiendish.

"We'll work on it," Nicole said. "Peter, you'll be Jared. And I'll be—no, Taylor, you can be Elizabeth."

"No, you're the actor in the family. I'm the writer," Taylor said. "I'll just narrate."

"You have to wear a period costume, too," Nicole said,

clearly happy to play Elizabeth. "Let's get our costumes. It helps your performance to be in the costume of a character, so we should start off that way." She pawed through the piles of clothes. "Cody, you need a Union uniform. That might be hard to find around here."

"My cousin was a Union soldier in a play. I can borrow his costume," Cody said.

"And I'll wear this!" Nicole held up a red satin southern belle dress with a huge skirt.

"I don't think Elizabeth would have worn red satin in the summer," Taylor said.

Nicole looked disappointed. "When was the shooting?"

Taylor looked at the printout. "June 25, 1862. A month after the battle."

"Today is June 25," Peter said.

CHAPTER
18

"IT'S THE ANNIVERSARY TONIGHT," NICOLE SAID IN HER SPECtral voice.

"We have to do something," Taylor said. "We have to correct something that isn't right. Tonight."

"Like what?" Peter said.

"What isn't right?" Cody said. "Jason tried to run away with his sweetheart and the gold, and he got caught and killed."

"I don't think it happened that way," Taylor said.

"Me either," Nicole said.

Nobody had any idea what else could have happened.

"Cody, you have to spend the night tonight," Peter said. "You have to be here for whatever is going to happen."

"I don't know. My mom said I've been living over here."

"Tell her you have to rehearse for the play. We only have a little over a week to get it ready."

He went off to call while Nicole looked for a dress.

"Try this one." Taylor held up a pale green one with yards and yards of ruffled skirt. "This is what she would have worn in summer. It'll be great with your green eyes."

"What are you going to wear?"

Taylor found a yellow dress. Nicole wanted to wear a straw bonnet but Taylor pointed out that the play happens at night. Peter found a gray coat that looked like a Confederate soldier's and said he could wear his own gray trousers and boots with a gold sash.

"Everybody get dressed and let's read through the lines," Nicole directed.

Taylor wiggled into the yellow dress. She didn't have a hoop to wear under it to hold the skirt out. The skirt spread at her feet so that it was like standing in a yellow pool. Nicole had a hoop, so hers belled around her legs, but it was still too long and she had to hold it up to keep from tripping.

Peter looked soldierly in his gray. Cody had draped a navy towel around himself.

Nicole placed everybody. "The visitors can stand in the dining room and parlor so they can see."

"Places, everybody." They all went upstairs, leaving Taylor at the foot.

"It is midnight, June 25, 1862," Taylor began. She read the story of the family: Abel Swain, who built the house on land that he fancied; Thomas, his descendant, and Thomas's daughter, Elizabeth; her cousins Jared and Jason Swain, orphaned brothers taken in by Thomas, who joined different sides in the Civil War. She read the story of the Battle of Winchester, of the wounded Jason recuperating at Swain's Fancy, of both brothers in love with Elizabeth.

"But one night Elizabeth slipped a note under Jason's door, a note asking him to meet her in the summerhouse. Jason thought she had chosen him. They would run away together, to Europe or South America. They would need money. He remembered Thomas Swain's hiding place, where he kept his gold. Perhaps Jason had discovered it by accident. Maybe he had seen Thomas putting money into his secret bank in the stairstep to the attic. He took the bag of gold downstairs and opened the front door to let his accomplice in, the accomplice he must have sent word to in the afternoon. He gave the bag of gold to the accomplice and went back for the other one, then ran with it down the stairs."

Cody as Jason ran downstairs, clutching a bag that looked suspiciously like Dad's shaving kit.

"But a noise awoke Jared. He ran downstairs as Jason was escaping from the house."

Peter as Jared ran down the stairs behind Cody.

"Jared couldn't see the thief's face. He saw only the back of the Union uniform, an enemy soldier. He raised his pistol and fired. The thief fell. Jared fired again but the accomplice thundered away on a horse. The household was aroused."

Nicole ran to the top of the stairs, peered down. "Oh no! What have you done?" She ran to the bottom of the stairs. "Is it? Oh no, it can't be." Nicole wasn't reading her lines—she had already memorized them. She ran to the fallen soldier and turned his face to the light from the lit candle she held.

"It's Jason. Oh, Jared, what have you done?"

"I have killed a thief," Peter read. "Look!" He kicked the leather pouch. "He has stolen your father's gold."

"There were two bags of gold," Taylor narrated.

"The accomplice got away with the other bag," Peter read.

"Oh, Jason, this can't be true," Nicole said, reaching out to the fallen Cody.

"Elizabeth refused to believe that Jason was a thief. She refused to marry Jared or anyone else. And for the rest of her life she searched for proof of Jason's innocence. She never found it. Now she walks the rooms of Swain's Fancy at night, still searching for proof. Someday, maybe she will find it.

"Brava! Bravo!" Dad and Sylvia stood at the door to the family room clapping enthusiastically.

"That's wonderful," Sylvia said. "You brilliant children! We'll get the paper to take some pictures. That will be terrific publicity for the tour. I'm sure somebody in the historical society has a replica of a pistol we can use. We'll have to alter the costumes and find a hoop for Taylor."

"Peter will have to memorize his lines," Nicole said. "But it's OK for Taylor to read hers. A narrator is sort of expected to read from something. It makes it seem more true."

"More true." Nicole's words rang in Taylor's mind. Something wasn't true. The ghost of Jason had had a gun every time they saw him. But the accounts said he didn't. Why wouldn't he if he was running away with the gold? Would he have had time to give it to the accomplice? Elizabeth believed Jason was innocent, but she never told anybody she was supposed to meet him at the summerhouse. Was that because it was against the rules in those days? And something else didn't ring true, but Taylor didn't know what it was.

The play was on. She had done her part. Now they had to practice it and get the costumes and the house ready. It would be a busy week.

But first, tonight, they had to go on a ghost watch.

After supper, after playing outside, after they were sent to bed, and after the grown-ups went to bed, they met in Peter's room to wait for midnight.

"What are we supposed to do?" Peter said.

"We're going to try to give the note to Elizabeth," Nicole said.

"What for? I mean what's that going to do?"

"Can you give something to a ghost?" Cody asked.

"I don't know," Nicole said.

"We want to see what she will do. I don't think she knows what she's looking for. She'll only know if she finds it," Taylor said. "She's always looked in the wrong places. When she sees the note, maybe it will remind her of something."

"Can a ghost read?" Peter asked.

"Guess we'll find out," Cody said.

"Or we can read it to her," Nicole said.

"What if Jason tries to shoot us again?" Peter didn't look happy about a ghost with a gun.

"He can't shoot us. He's a ghost," Nicole said.

"I'm not going to bet on it," Cody said.

Taylor wasn't so sure either. But she was sure that Jason thought he could shoot them. And he would surely threaten to if they tried to give the note to Elizabeth. She wiped her sweaty palms on her shorts.

"If we give the note to the ghost and she takes it, we won't have it anymore," Peter said.

"I made copies this afternoon," Taylor said.

"It's getting close to time," Cody said.

They looked at each other. Then Nicole stood up, and they followed into her room. They sat against the wall out of the way. Taylor held the note between her two fingers and waited as Nicole turned off the lamp. Their eyes adjusted to the dark. In a few minutes Elizabeth glided in. She wore the dark dress, her hair pulled severely back. She had lines on her forehead. She didn't look young as she wrung her hands.

Then she was gone.

Nicole turned on the light. "I thought you were going to give her the note."

"She's old. I want to give it to the young Elizabeth in the nightgown that we saw at the séance."

"Why? Just give it to her and let's get these ghosts to stop walking around our house," Peter said.

Taylor didn't know why. "Maybe it will change some-thing," she said.

They moved across the hall to the antique bedroom. They stopped at the door. Nobody wanted to go in. "Come on," Taylor said. "We've found the note. It shouldn't matter to Jason. He can't stop us now," Nicole said.

"That's right. The note isn't there anymore. The old Eliza-beth will come, and then Jason. But he may not come if we're not there. Let's wait in the hall instead and see what happens out here," Taylor suggested.

They could also escape to the safety of Peter's room more quickly from the hall, so everybody agreed. They sat on the floor in front of his door.

"This is more exciting," Cody said.

"Yeah," Peter agreed. "I was getting tired of those ghosts doing the same old thing all the time. They need reprogram-ming."

Taylor opened her mouth to say that you can't program ghosts when the figure of a man in a blue uniform emerged from the antique bedroom. He had no gun, no pouch. He didn't go to the attic stairs where the gold was kept, but instead ran lightly down the steps to the hall below. He looked happy. Another soldier in blue ran after him. He had a gun and carried what looked like a leather bag.

Now Taylor was confused. The icy ghost they'd thought was Jason was really Jared. Jason *was* innocent.

"He's got the gold!" Peter whispered.

"Quick, follow them," Nicole said.

They raced to the top of the stairs in time to see Jared raise the gun, and without calling "Halt!" or saying a word, he fired. The bullet hit Jason in the back. He fell soundlessly onto the rag rug, a red bloom of blood expanding on the back of his blue uniform. Jared stepped over him and opened the door. Without aiming, he fired into the dark outside. Then he shoved the pouch under his brother and hurriedly searched his pockets.

Now Taylor knew what she had been trying to think of all day.

"You can't wear the green dress, Nicole," she whispered.

"What?"

"Elizabeth ran downstairs in her nightgown at the séance. She wore a nightgown that night in 1862 when she was young, and she'll be wearing one tonight."

As she spoke, a woman ran down the stairs, her long white nightgown trailing behind her. At the bottom the young Elizabeth stopped, staring at Jared, who had stood up when he heard her and was still holding the pistol. She fell to her knees and turned Jason over.

Now. Now was the moment to give the note to Elizabeth.

CHAPTER

19

TAYLOR WOULD NEVER FORGET THE SCENE. JASON LAY DEAD ON a rug stretched across the doorway. Elizabeth held his head in her lap. Jared stood over them, his arms by his side, pistol smoking as it pointed at the floor.

Jared turned as Taylor approached them with the note in her hand. He looked straight at her. He saw her. The eyes of a man dead for more than a century looked into Taylor's. They blazed with a blinding blue light in the ghostly darkness. His mouth opened in a hideous snarl. He raised the gun.

Taylor walked toward the boots of the fallen Jason. Her knees felt like they were going to collapse under her. She had to reach Elizabeth. Each step seemed to take forever. Jared sighted the pistol. She couldn't make it. He aimed at a point between her eyes.

Someone was with her—Nicole on one side, Peter and Cody on the other.

"He can't shoot us all," Peter said.

"Give her the note," Nicole said.

"Hurry," Cody added.

There wasn't much time. The ghosts could fade away at any moment. Taylor leaned as far as she could over the dead Jason, the note in her hand.

"Elizabeth," Taylor whispered, "Jason was going to meet you. He thought you had sent this note asking you to meet him in the summerhouse. Jared stole the gold. There was no accomplice. Jared planted the gold underneath Jason. He kept the rest for himself. He must have stashed it somewhere and gotten it later."

Jared's ghost seemed to grow larger with rage. His ice-blue eyes stared like gun barrels at Taylor. His mouth opened in a soundless yell of rage as he pulled the trigger. Just at that moment, Elizabeth stood up. She hit Jared's arm, deflecting his aim. The pistol shot sounded as loud as a cannon in the entrance hall.

Elizabeth held her hand out to Taylor, who passed her the note. Their fingers brushed, but Taylor didn't recoil. She wasn't sure she felt Elizabeth's touch like the soft tips of a bird's wing or if she imagined it. Elizabeth looked down at the note as she read it. Then she turned to Jared, her face filled with loathing and contempt. He backed away from her, the pistol still hanging at his side. His mouth formed the word "no."

And then Jared was gone, the pixels of blue-white light diminishing until there was nothing left and he was dissolved into nothingness, leaving Elizabeth and the ghost of Jason's corpse on the rug. Then Jason stirred and rose. He held his arm out for Elizabeth. She took it, and they walked through the front door into the dark. Elizabeth looked back at Taylor, and as their eyes locked, she nodded her head. The note fluttered to the floor.

"Wow!" Peter spoke for all of them.

"She was thanking you," Nicole said.

"Where are they going?" Cody asked.

They ran to the window and watched as Elizabeth and Jason walked across the bridge to the summerhouse and faded into the moonlight.

"Jason was innocent," Peter said. "He never had a gun."

"It was Jared all the time. He was the evil brother, not Jason as everybody thought. He wrote the note," Nicole said.

"How did you know, Taylor?" Cody asked.

"Elizabeth was wearing a nightgown the night Jason was killed just as she did when we saw her at the séance. If Elizabeth had sent Jason a note to meet her, she would have worn a dress, not a nightgown. They may have been planning to elope. Jared must have overheard and decided on a plan to get rid of his rival and steal Thomas Swain's gold at the same time. That's how I knew Elizabeth didn't know about the note."

"You were right. She's been searching for something all these years, and she didn't even know what it was," Nicole said.

"Neither did we," Taylor said.

"But you solved it," Nicole said.

"You solved it, too," Taylor said. "If you hadn't played that trick with Abel Swain's head, you wouldn't have signed the note that fell behind the baseboard. If we hadn't been looking for it, we never would have found Jared's note."

"It was a collaboration," Peter said.

They looked at each other, and Taylor wondered if they were thinking what she was—that collaboration was the way to get things done. Like the reenactment that she would now have to rewrite.

CHAPTER
20

THE NEXT WEEK WAS A BLUR OF REHEARSALS, COSTUME fittings, and newspaper photographers, interspersed with washing windows, walls, floors, and furniture. Sylvia finally declared that Swain's Fancy was ready for the July Daze Festival. At Goodwill they found a rag rug in the same colors as the ghost rug to use for the play. The festival was scheduled for the weekend after the Fourth of July. Cody's parents invited them to come over for a cookout and picnic on the Fourth. Sylvia, Nicole, and Taylor baked Sylvia's red velvet cake for their contribution. It was a lot of work. Taylor had never made a cake from scratch before; Mom didn't have a lot of time to cook at home. It was fun with all three making it together.

"Since it's your first time, Taylor, you get to pour in the red food coloring. That's what makes the cake like red velvet."

Taylor looked doubtfully at the chocolate cake batter. She didn't see how anything could make that dark stuff change color. But she poured the whole bottle of red coloring in, and they took turns with the electric mixer. Taylor was amazed when they removed the three pans of cake layers from the oven an hour later.

"It looks just like red velvet!" she said.

"Of course." Sylvia said. "Culinary magic."

They iced it with white cream-cheese frosting. Then the cooks licked the bowl. "Yummy," Taylor said.

Cody lived in a sprawling old two-story farmhouse. His relatives had come for the holiday, and the house swarmed with Jacksons of all ages, including Cody's two little brothers, Tom and George. When the relatives heard about the play Cody was in, they all said they would come to see it. "There may not be room for anybody else," they joked. "This valley is full of Jacksons."

Opening day for the July Daze Festival was overcast when Taylor woke up in Nicole's room. Nicole had insisted that they share the room and her bed until the new rooms were created in the attic.

"It's more fun to share," Nicole said. "And be like real sisters."

"I always wanted a sister," Taylor said. "I'm glad you're my sister now." They would probably have fights and fusses in the future. All sisters that Taylor had ever heard of did. But now they were connected, and they would get over it. They would share her dad and Sylvia, too. And Taylor had her

148

own mother to share when Nicole and Peter came to visit her in Washington.

They helped each other dress in their costumes and went downstairs. They had decided that Nicole should wear the green dress and the straw bonnet and change into the nightgown just before time to perform. It meant a lot of changing, but Nicole didn't mind. "It's what actors love to do," she said. Besides, she didn't want to have to wear the white nightgown all day. Taylor knew Nicole wanted to dress up in the hoop skirt and pantaloons underneath the full-skirted green dress and the bonnet with the green ribbons, and flounce around like a belle. Taylor wore the yellow dress, which Sylvia had taken up to fit her.

Taylor had stood on a stool while Sylvia pinned up the skirt so it wouldn't drag on the floor. The pantaloons were hot, but at least the hoop kept the skirt away from her legs.

"I'm glad I don't have to wear this stuff all the time," Taylor had said.

Sylvia had laughed through a mouthful of pins. She stuck them in the hem. "Me, too. They also wore corsets so tight their insides were moved around and squished up. On top of that they wore corset covers, shifts, a hoop, and umpteen petticoats. That's why stairways in the houses built in that period had couches on the landings halfway up the stairs."

"Why?" Nicole had asked. "So they could sit down and rest?"

"Well, that too, but they were called fainting couches

because the ladies would often faint after the least exertion. For some, it was halfway up the stairs."

"Yuck," Taylor had said.

"Double that," Nicole agreed.

Taylor didn't want breakfast this morning. She wasn't wearing corset covers and shifts and petticoats, but Sylvia had made the top of the yellow dress a snug fit. She didn't want to gain an ounce before the play.

Sylvia convinced her she needed the energy, so Taylor ate a buttered English muffin while Nicole nibbled a dry bagel. Cody came over in his Union uniform as they were finishing. He had borrowed a replica of a Civil War pistol that shot caps.

The performances would be on the hour, starting at ten. In between the actors were stationed around the house in different rooms. Some of the rooms were off-limits to visitors: Nicole's, Peter's, the bathroom, the cellar, the family wing. But the hall upstairs and down, parlor, dining room, and antique bedroom were on view. In the program Sylvia had written that in the future they hoped to have more of the house on view, but they had only owned the house for six months and these rooms were the only ones they'd managed to have ready so far.

At ten they took their stations as the visitors gathered in the downstairs room to watch the first performance of the play. Nicole, Peter, and Cody went upstairs, leaving Taylor alone at the bottom. She stood on the side of the stairway and cleared her throat. Taylor felt shaky. She had memorized her part but she pretended to read it as if from a book.

"It is midnight, June 25, 1862," she began. "Jared and Jason Swain, brothers and the wards of Thomas Swain, owner of Swain's Fancy, were both in love with Elizabeth, Thomas Swain's daughter. Elizabeth had grown up with both of them and loved both but she could marry only one, and she couldn't decide which. The brothers, once close, were now rivals for Elizabeth. The Civil War, which had begun in April 1861, drove them further apart. The Eastern Panhandle of what became West Virginia was divided between Union and Confederate. Thomas Swain was a Quaker. He refused to take sides in the war, but the brothers did. Jared joined the Confederate army, as three-fourths of the men in the area did. Jason joined the Union."

"On the twenty-fifth of May, 1862, General Stonewall Jackson attacked the Union army under General Nathaniel Banks in Winchester, Virginia. Jackson and General Early forced the Union troops to fall back to Harper's Ferry. Jason Swain was wounded in the battle. He made it back to Swain's Fancy, where Thomas took him in. While Jason was getting well, Elizabeth realized that he was the brother she loved. They had just decided to marry when Jared, learning that his brother was here, came to capture him and remove him from Elizabeth's presence. Thomas refused to allow that to happen. 'There will be no war at Swain's Fancy,' he told his wards.

151

"The brothers abided by Thomas's decree, but on that June night a month after the battle, Jared was desperate to break up the romance. He wanted Elizabeth for himself. He wrote a note to Jason asking him to meet Elizabeth in the summerhouse on the pond. He signed it with Elizabeth's initial." Taylor held up the note, which Dad had placed in a plastic cover to protect it.

Cody came down the stairs. Nicole had coached him in his part. He looked happy and excited, the way Jason had looked running down the stairs on his way to meet his beloved Elizabeth.

Just as he reached the rag rug in front of the door, Peter ran down the stairs, a leather bag in his left hand, his right hand stretched out in front of him, holding a pistol that was aimed at Cody.

"Blam!" Several people jumped when the cap pistol went off. Cody fell facedown on the rug.

Peter opened the front door and shot again. Then he shoved the bag under the fallen Jason and began to search the pockets of his uniform.

Suddenly the hall was filled with a loud shriek. "Noooo!"

Taylor and everybody else jerked their eyes to the top of the stairs. A barefoot Nicole stood there in a long white cotton nightgown with lace inserts, her hand to her mouth, her eyes wild with fear. "Jared! What have you done?"

Peter as Jared jumped to his feet. He twisted his mouth the way he had seen the real Jared do it.

This time the incident they enacted told the truth about Jared's treachery, his murder of his brother, his theft of the gold, and Elizabeth's faithfulness—never marrying, searching for proof of Jason's innocence.

As she read, Taylor thought she knew why Swain's Fancy had never been reported as haunted. Nobody had ever seen the ghosts. Elizabeth's search and Jared's jealous rivalry had fed off the energy from *them*—from Taylor's search for a place in this new blended family, from her rivalry with Nicole. Elizabeth had probably searched since that night in 1862, but she was such a gentle ghost she hadn't been noticed. Until they got close to the note, Jared hadn't appeared. Once she and Nicole started using that room, he had to appear to try to frighten them away. They were a danger to the story that people had believed since 1862. Jared didn't want the truth known. He especially didn't want Elizabeth to know it. Not even after death.

Taylor ended with Elizabeth's search for proof of Jason's innocence. "She searched for the rest of her life, but she never found the note that Jared had forged—the note found this summer behind the baseboard where it had fallen on that warm June night in 1862."

The crowd clapped and whistled as the three actors and the narrator took their bows. Nicole said they were a little stiff, but they loosened up by the second performance.

The audiences had a lot of questions about the house, the people who lived there, the play.

"Is this true?" asked a woman in a big floppy hat.

"Are you professional actors?" a man wanted to know.

They posed for pictures. One couple took a whole roll of film of them. "Are you all sisters and brothers?" the husband asked.

"Yes," Taylor said. "This is my sister, Nicole, and my brother, Peter, and our friend Cody from next door."

Someone from a little theater asked them to try out for the next play in Martinsburg. The Burneytown librarian, Mrs. Mills, wanted them to perform the play at the library. And there were other invitations to perform their play at club meetings and even a garden party.

Nicole bubbled with plans for more plays. "Taylor can write them. I'll direct, and Cody and Peter can produce. We'll all star in them."

They would collaborate. Suddenly, collaborating all summer at Swain's Fancy seemed like the most fun in the world to Taylor.